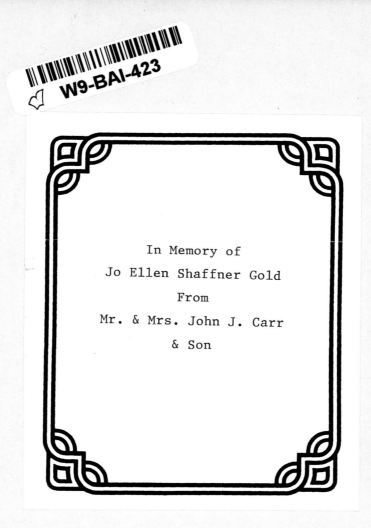

In Memory of
Jo Ellen Shaffner Gold
From
Mr. & Mrs. John J. Carr
& Son

Legend
of the
Island Horse

JENNY HUGHES

BREAKAWAY BOOKS
HALCOTTSVILLE, NEW YORK
2013

ISBN: 978-1-62124-007-5
Library of Congress Control Number: 2013945595

Published by Breakaway Books
P.O. Box 24
Halcottsville, NY 12438
www.breakawaybooks.com

NOTE: For this edition, we have Americanized the spellings (for instance "color" instead of "colour"), but kept the original British vocabulary and usage. So, for anyone not familiar with some of these terms, here is a brief list with their American equivalents: rosettes= ribbons; downs=open fields with rolling hills; mate=friend; copse= a small group of trees; head collar=a horse's halter; numnah=saddle pad; school=riding ring; yard=stable area.

10 9 8 7 6 5 4 3 2 1

Chapter One

The ship tossed and bucketed through towering waves on the storm-lashed sea, her sails torn into useless, tattered rags by the merciless, raging wind. Her crew fought to regain control, soaked in rain and salt spray, their bare feet slipping on the flooded deck, their voices lost in the howling maelstrom. Above the roar of the storm came the crashing of sea on rock as the mighty waves smashed again and again on a jagged, jutting outcrop. The ship spun skyward on the crest of such a giant and was hurled down again to splinter like matchwood on the rocks. The horse, terrified and panicking belowdecks, was catapulted into the icy heaving water as the rope halter tethering him snapped like cotton thread. There was nothing except the storm howling around him, the black depths surging and sucking him under while the rain and wind lashed him from above. He struck out strongly, throwing his head high as he swam, his legs pumping hard below the savage waves, feel-

ing himself tossed and battered but fighting, fighting all the way. Just as it seemed he could not hold on, that his tired legs would no longer keep him afloat, the sea's fury abated slightly and the vicious current, instead of pulling him down, pushed him forward. He had no way of knowing he'd reached a sheltered bay on the Island of Morvona; all he knew was that his hooves touched land and at last he was able to stagger from the cruel, raging sea. The legend of the Island Horse had begun.

"What d'you think?" Dad was watching my face. "Does it make you want to read on?"

"Oh sure." I turned away from the computer screen to smile at him. "But you know me, I'd read a cereal box if it had a horse on it."

"Thanks a lot, Tia!" He pulled a mock-crying face. "I wonder why I don't ask your opinion of my writing more often."

"It's great, Dad." I picked up a tissue and pretended to dry his pretend tears. "And you don't me show me your stuff because you hate anyone reading your books until they're published."

"True," he agreed. "I feel quite secretive while I'm actually working on something, but seeing that this new one is going to be centered around a horse, and you're the most horse-oriented person I have ever known, I wanted to know what you thought."

"Good. I think it's good. But it seems like an odd choice of subject for you. Even though I've had Gable for four years, you're still not sure which end is which!"

Gable is the love of my life, a beautiful nine-year-old Quarter Horse, the color of polished teak. I spend practically every waking minute with him, and although Dad is highly supportive and encouraging, watching every competition we enter, he's never shown any inclination to get involved himself. He'll give Gable a kindly pat and a whole tube of his favorite sweets but that's as far as it goes, so I was quite surprised about the subject matter of this new novel. All his other books have had historical settings and are full of gritty realism, so making up a story about a legendary horse was a real departure from the norm. I said as much and he became very animated, rifling through a mess of old papers on his untidy desk.

"The thing is, I'm not inventing it, the story will be based on a shipwreck that actually did happen off the English coast a hundred and fifty years ago. Everyone aboard perished except this one horse, who swam ashore and lived as a wild stallion on the island."

"Fantastic!" I love stuff like that. "But I still can't see you writing a whole novel about a horse."

"My angle will be the power struggle between two rival families on Morvona, with the horse being the catalyst that reignites an old feud." Dad's eyes were gleaming at the thought.

"Right," I said, trying to sound as if I got it.

"The trouble is"—he peered over the top of his glasses to look at one of the papers—"I can't find any real evidence that the horse *did* actually exist. It seems to be just handed-down folklore. I'd really like to see some documentation that would imbue my novel with that authentic ring."

I enjoy it when he talks to me as if I'm a grown-up on the same level. We're really, really close; my mum died eight years ago when I was only seven so Dad's been everything to me. Of course it's been mostly on the him-looking-after-me basis, so it's great now that I'm older we've started discussing things like equals.

Now I said, "Well, even if you can't find proof of the Island Horse it sounds like a good idea for a story."

"Mm." He obviously didn't agree. "I need to do more research, and since I've exhausted the Internet and the library it only leaves the actual location—Morvona itself."

"The island?" I stared at him. "But it's miles away— oh, surely you're not going over there and leaving me with Aunt Jo?"

Aunt Jo's our only other family member. She's actually Dad's aunty, so she must be about a hundred.

"No, I hadn't planned to do that." He hesitated and I felt a funny shudder wondering if he was considering leaving me on my own. That would be exciting in its way but pretty scary.

"There's a cottage I can rent, and I thought I'd take you with me." He wasn't making eye contact so I knew he wasn't sure how I'd react.

"Skip school?" I was well up for it. "Yeah definitely."

"Behave yourself, Tia Carberry." This was said in his

mock stern I'm-a-proper-father voice. "I meant in the summer holidays of course."

"Dad!" I couldn't believe my ears. "You know I want to spend the vacation practicing cross-country with Gable. We've got that big competition in September."

"We'd only be in Morvona a week or two." He looked at my stony expression. "Three at the most. Don't forget Kate's away for a month too."

Kate is my best friend, owner of a loony chestnut mare called Tallulah.

"I know she is, but that doesn't stop me and Gable from practicing. And anyway, who's going to look after him if I go?"

"Don't the people at the livery yard do it?" Dad's pretty vague sometimes, and I felt a nasty stab of resentment.

"I don't want just anyone for Gable. You're only thinking about yourself. You don't care about me and my pony!"

"Tia, love." He took off his glasses and rubbed his eyes tiredly. "The books are my job; they supply the money for you *and* for Gable. I know you don't like staying with

Aunt Jo so I thought it'd be nice to visit the island together."

Although I recognized this as perfectly reasonable I'd worked myself up into a rage and wouldn't respond, stomping out of his office and out through our back door. My bike was still lying on the grass where I'd dumped it after school and I wrenched it off the ground and jumped aboard, ignoring Dad's voice calling me back. I pedaled furiously, with my long dark hair streaming out behind me, through our small village; I turned right at the crossroads and within five minutes was walking across the flower-studded grass of Gable's meadow. He shares his field with three other ponies, and they all looked up from their grazing as I stamped bad-temperedly by. Gable was on the very far side, dozing contentedly under the shade of a big maple tree. He was lying down, not flat out as he did at night, but with his legs curled beneath his gently nodding head. I knelt beside him and put my arms round his neck, breathing in his lovely sweet smell.

"Oh Gable." I cuddled into him, feeling his velvety lips brush my arm. "Dad wants me to go to some stupid island to find out about some stupid horse for his stupid, stupid book."

Not exactly the fairest or most intelligent summary of the situation but I was feeling sorry for myself.

"I told him I didn't want to leave you so I bet he gets old Jo to look after me. She's the one who cooks everything till it's soggy and thinks I should be in bed by eight."

Gable blew softly his nose in sympathy. Yeah, all right, he doesn't understand exactly what I'm saying but he knows when I'm upset and he's always, always on my side. I ranted on for ages about Dad being inconsiderate and tried not to listen to a small voice inside my head that said I was being pretty selfish and unreasonable myself. After a while even Gable got bored and gently nudged me out of the way so he could get to his feet and start grazing again. He hadn't actually offered any advice, of course, but being with him was kind of calming and uplifting at the same time so I made my mind up to go home and give my hardworking dad the support he deserved. One of the other girls who kept her pony at the yard was really nice, and I was sure she'd be willing to care for Gable while Dad and I were away on Morvona.

"We'll just have to do double the cross-country practice when I get back," I told Gable, giving him a final good-bye kiss, and he whickered solemnly as if in agreement.

I pedaled back home and walked quietly back to Dad's office door. I could hear him talking to someone on the phone so waited before I went in.

"That's great," he said, sounding relieved. "Tia really doesn't want to be parted from her horse so I'm very grateful to you. Very grateful indeed."

No! the voice inside my head screamed. *Now you've done it, Tia—Dad's gone and booked Aunt Jo to stay here with you while he goes to the island!*

I very nearly stamped off again but stuck my head round the door instead. "Sorry I threw a tantrum." I made myself smile at him.

Dad turned toward me and returned the smile immediately. "That's okay, honey. I should have thought about Gable, but my head was so full of the Island Horse story it just wasn't working on a practical level." He rose to his full height—over six feet—and gave me a hug, adding,

"But it's all right now. I've fixed it."

I shut my eyes briefly, waiting for him to tell me the worst.

"Dead simple really, there's a paddock right next to the cottage and everything." He clicked on the computer and printed out a picture. "Look, Tia. I reckon even the best horse in the world—that's Gable, obviously—will like a few weeks' holiday here."

He held up the paper and I found myself gaping at a quaint stone-built cottage set in the middle of rolling hills and lush green fields.

"There's Gable's paddock." Dad pointed proudly. "It's got a shelter and everything *and* you'll be able to see him from your bedroom window—how perfect is that?"

"*Absolutely* perfect." He looked so anxious I thought I ought to put his mind at rest. "Will the weather be good too?"

"Well, nothing's guaranteed—you know Great Britain! Morvona's off the south coast, but it's climate is still changeable." He peered at yet more notes. "It can be hot and sunny in the summer months but it's subject to storms."

"Sunny sounds great—I might even get a tan. Thanks, Dad, I'm really looking forward to it."

That wasn't strictly true, in fact, because although I was a million times happier about the trip now Gable was coming with us, the thought of weeks spent on a remote island didn't exactly fill me with joy. Where we live is quiet but it's not far from town, so there are great shops and cinemas and always loads of friends to hang out with, whereas on Morvona I was going to be mooching around all on my own. Still, like Dad said, writing books was his job, this was part of his job and I felt I had to be supportive.

I kept up a good show of enthusiasm for the next few weeks. When the day finally arrived we had to make an early start, and as usual I spent twice as long getting Gable and all his paraphernalia ready as I did throwing my own T-shirts and stuff into a bag.

"Don't forget a couple of swimsuits," Dad called out. "Morvona's got a rocky coastline but there's bound to be somewhere to swim."

I hadn't done much swimming in the sea—we live inland—so I must admit I felt quite a thrill of excitement when Dad pulled up at the ferry terminal and there was the ocean sparkling before us. The long trip had meant stopping overnight, and since then I'd taken Gable out of his trailer to stretch his legs and have a drink before embarking on his first sea trip. I knew he was comfortable but couldn't wait for Dad to drive aboard so I could climb into the trailer and see my pony's reaction. It was a bit disappointing: Gable was so laid-back he hardly flicked an ear as the big ferry churned slowly out of the harbor. By the time we'd reached the open sea he was calmly munching at his hay net, completely ignoring the strange new scenery sliding by outside. I, on the other hand, was acting like a four-year-old, running along the deck to watch from as many different angles as I could. We were gliding smoothly across a calm sea that gleamed silver-blue under the summer sun. I gazed into the creamy, frothing wake made by our progress and tried to imagine this same ocean black and heaving with the violence of a storm.

"We should get our first glimpse of Morvona soon." Dad came and leaned over the side with me. "I'm told it appears to rise out of the sea and—oh look, there it is!"

I screwed up my eyes against the sun and saw a jagged emerald dot on the horizon.

"That's miles away." I'd imagined it much closer to the mainland. "Where are the rocks that caused the shipwreck, Dad? I want to see how far your Island Horse swam."

"You can't see from here. We're approaching the southern side where the ferry port is. It's the rockier northern end where the story's based."

So the rocky north was where we headed, driving out of the busy, noisy port along green-fringed country roads, which grew narrower and bumpier as we went along. Dad negotiated each twist and turn with care, maneuvering Gable's trailer as smoothly as he could, eventually pausing at the summit of a hill.

"There." He pulled on the hand brake and pointed down, his other hand tracing the route on a map. "Rockrose Cottage—our home for the next week or two."

I peered eagerly out of the window and caught my breath. The little house was certainly quaint, its roof furry with moss, its stone walls smothered in rambling roses, but it was even more remote than I'd feared.

"It looks like the only building in the valley," I said. "There's nothing else at all."

"They said there was a farm nearby." Dad reached for his binoculars. "We can get our fresh food there."

"Yeah, if we put out hiking boots on!" I took the field glasses, put them to my eyes, and adjusted the sights. "No, there's nothing. Absolutely noth—" I stopped abruptly, feeling my heart make an extraordinary pounding lurch.

There, on the brow of the hill above Rockrose Cottage, was a horse and rider. The horse's classy lines gleamed a true ebony black, matching almost exactly the dark, windswept hair of the great-looking boy astride him. Suddenly the idea of riding Gable though this wild and lonely landscape became something I really, *really* couldn't wait to do!

Chapter Two

The cottage, when we reached it, was lovely, and someone had left a welcome in the form of fresh flowers, crusty bread, and a bowl of apples.

"There's milk and eggs in the fridge too." Dad was unpacking the food he'd brought. "That's a nice touch."

"Yeah." I figured the gorgeous horse rider probably came from the farm and was secretly disappointed I now couldn't offer to ride over there to fetch provisions. Still, there was plenty of time to call on the neighbors; my immediate priority was to get Gable settled in. I told Dad as much and he grinned.

"First things first, right? I thought you might like something to eat but obviously not until you and that horse of yours have inspected every blade of grass in his new paddock."

"You don't need a hand, do you?" I was practically out of the door before he could wave peaceably and say, "No, I'm fine."

Gable, as usual, had traveled brilliantly and was now curious to see where we were. He walked calmly down the trailer's ramp and lowered his head to sniff at a patch of clover by the gate. I let him take his time, holding his lead rope and walking with him so he'd stretch out his legs but not go charging around like a maniac. He's a very laid-back pony but like most horses gets overexcited with a new experience sometimes, and I didn't want him injuring himself. The paddock was a good size and was well fenced with a self-filling water trough. The grazing was good, but not so lush it would turn my athletic boy into a fatty, and the three-sided shelter was stoutly built. I wasn't worried about Gable living on his own: Although he likes being with his friends at home he's got quite a solitary streak and never worries when they go out.

"Anyway"—I pulled his copper-colored ears gently—"hopefully you'll be getting company when we go out. We should be getting to know a couple of handsome dark strangers so that's something to look forward to."

He blew down his nose and gave me his friendly nudge of agreement. Seeing how calm he was, I took off his head collar and let him go exploring on his own. He moved off, head and tail high so that his mane and tail flowed like banners, his steps lengthening until he was sailing across the grass in a perfect extended trot. He looked like the finest kind of show horse till he stopped, put his head down, and pawed at the ground, turning round like a dog making a bed. His knees and hocks bent and, smiling, I waited for him to roll—but he changed his mind and moved to another drier and dustier patch, where at last he sagged down with a grunt of pleasure. Over he went, balancing on his spine, and I laughed to see the seam where his coat meets on his stomach and the flash of silver as his hooves waved happily in the air. I'd watched him roll hundreds of times before but I always loved to see the sheer joy he got as he thumped down on one side, squirming ecstatically to get as much ground contact as possible before repeating the whole ritual on the other side. Once satisfied he got up, planted his feet squarely, and shook from head to tail, sending showers of dust and lumps of earth flying into the clean, fragrant air.

I think apart from the physical pleasure horses get from rolling, it helps them feel they've made their mark on their surroundings. Gable certainly seemed settled as he dropped his head to crop the grass contentedly. I watched him for a while longer then hopped back over the gate that led directly into Rockrose Cottage's garden. Dad had finished unpacking the car and called out that he'd put my bag in the first bedroom off the upstairs landing, so I hurtled up there to put my stuff away. It didn't take long, only ten minutes or so, and about nine of those were spent looking out the window at Gable as he wandered peacefully around the paddock directly below.

"I've made some sandwiches," Dad called up. "D'you want one, Tia?"

Although we'd had a snack on the ferry I'd been too hyped up to eat much and now realized I was starving, so I ran down to join him. We took our plates into the slightly wild but very pretty back garden. We sat munching happily, with Dad looking around at the scenery with great interest while I watched my pony. Although he seemed perfectly fine I decided not to ride him till the next day.

"I'm giving Gable the rest of the day off to really settle in," I told Dad. "So what d'you want to do—start researching your horse legend? I'll help if you like."

"I've done enough driving for the day so I think I'll just get my bearings and find out where the farm is and if the coast is in easy walking distance."

"Are we near the sea then?" I was surprised, thinking I'd hear waves crashing and all that, but the little valley was pure countryside, just birdsong, trees, and grass.

"Not far." Dad spread his map out again and pointed. Morvona was shaped roughly like an arrowhead with the broad part at the south where we'd landed, narrowing to the pointy bit where we were now. The cottage was just off center at the northern end, and it was quite exciting for a landlocked person like me to realize I was now living only a few miles from the ocean with coastlines to the north, east, and west from where I was sitting. Dad and I went for a stroll later, climbing the hill behind the cottage to the ridge where I'd seen the black horse. We could see a farm, which was just over the edge of our skyline, and I guessed it wouldn't take more than ten or fifteen minutes of riding to reach it, though Dad thought it was quite a walk.

"I can drive the road way instead," he said. "It must be the farm that the owners of Rockrose told us about. They seem friendly, judging by how nicely they stocked the cottage. At least I hope so, anyway."

Picturing the good-looking rider I'd seen through the binoculars I fervently agreed, only under my breath naturally. Dad and I were gradually developing a more grown-up relationship, like I say, but I wasn't ready to discuss potential boyfriends yet. We spent an enjoyable, relaxed kind of evening and it was great being able to just walk to the paddock fence to say good night to my pony. The morning started well too, being able to see Gable as soon as I opened my eyes, and eating breakfast in the garden only a few feet away from where he grazed. Unfortunately as soon as I went to get my grooming kit and tack, a bit of a row broke out between Dad and me.

"Leave your riding till later, will you please, Tia?" He was quickly clearing plates. "I want to go into Redhaven—that's the nearest town—and check out their local records."

"But I don't," I said, conveniently forgetting my offer of help the day before. "I want to ride Gable to the coast."

"Not on your own you can't. You don't know your way around, you could get lost."

"Don't be silly," I argued. "You showed me the map—it's only a short distance to the cliffs in the west. I'll show you the route we'll take and I'll be back at lunchtime."

"It's not safe on your own," he repeated.

"Oh Dad!" I was exasperated. "I've been riding alone for years. I'll take my cell phone and I promise to be careful. You didn't expect to come everywhere with me and Gable this holiday surely?"

"I thought I could follow on my mountain bike when you ride out. And I also thought you'd come with me to libraries and so on."

"Now, that *would* be a laugh, wouldn't it!" I stuck out my lower lip, knowing how much he hates it when I sulk.

"Come on, you do your thing this morning and I'll do mine and we can join up later and tell each other how it went."

"Let me see the route you're going to take then." He knew I'd keep on till I got my own way.

"Okay." I traced a trail from the cottage, skirting the farm (only I intended calling in there, obviously!) then following a track that led the few miles to the coast.

"I suppose it's all right." Dad sighed and picked up his own cell phone. "Call me to check in."

"Yep." I leaned over and kissed his cheek lightly. "Stop worrying. I hope you have a good time and find out loads about the legend."

"Thanks and—er—don't go too fast but be back here by one o'clock."

"Sure." I waved cheerily and went into Gable's field.

My horse had a lot of dust for me to remove, but he was looking well rested. As soon as we set off I knew he was as keen as I was to get going. Once he was warmed up we found an inviting, upward-sloping track of springy turf and I gave him the aids for canter. He surged forward joyfully, and we were soon approaching the big double gates of the farm. As I hesitated, wondering what excuse I could use to call in, an ancient jeep clattered toward us and a fair-haired woman waved out the window.

"Hi. You must be from Rockrose."

"Yes. Hello, I'm Tia. Um—I was just going to say thanks for the flowers and bread and everything."

"You're very welcome. I'm off to Redhaven but my husband's around if you want more eggs or anything."

"No, we're fine, thank you." It wouldn't be cool to say *Was that your good-looking son I saw riding his gorgeous horse and would he be home by any chance?* would it, so I just waved again and she drove off.

I walked Gable along the hard-baked track till we had the softer turf beneath us again and we enjoyed another brisk canter. We were riding through fairly gentle, pretty scenery, following a line of fencing that must have been the farm's perimeter, but gradually as we left that behind the terrain grew wilder and I could smell the faint, tantalizing tang of the sea. We were still gradually climbing, a broad sweep of grass curving away into the distance, and

I felt Gable prance a little as he shared my excitement. It was the perfect place for a gallop and my pony responded immediately, lengthening his stride into the exciting four-beat rhythm. I could taste the salt flavor of the wind in my face; my hair, long and loose under my riding hat, streamed around my shoulders as we raced across the short springy turf. I knew how a bird in flight must feel and was aware Gable could feel it too, that glorious sense of power and freedom.

At the top of the slope the track straightened and I caught my breath at the stunning view to our left. We were now galloping along the top of the cliff; the sea, more turbulent and a deeper blue than yesterday, moved endlessly below us. I brought the pace down, slowing Gable gradually until he came to a halt so I could turn him and stare out, fascinated, at the great, restless mass of water. Gable looked too, his fine dark eyes taking in the unfamiliar beauty, his nostrils flaring gently. I was so mesmerized I didn't hear the other horse's approach; it was only when my pony turned and whickered softly that I became aware we weren't alone. The black horse moved beautifully and his rider sat with an almost arrogant air of complete assurance, but his dark eyes were friendly as he raised a hand in greeting.

"Hi. We watched you gallop up the hill—that horse of yours can sure motor."

"He's pretty fast," I agreed, again experiencing my heart perform a trampoline-type leap. "He's called Gable and I'm Tia. We're staying—"

"At Rockrose Cottage. Yeah I know, I'm Daniel Creech and I live at Tarag House, about half a mile from here. My mum said she heard someone was bringing their pony on holiday to the cottage."

So he wasn't the farmers' son. "Oh right. Er—I think I saw you on the ridge yesterday." I sounded pretty cool, I thought. "Your horse is a stunner, isn't he?"

"Harley? He's not bad, I guess."

Hearing the unmistakable note of besotted pride that afflicts us horse owners, I paid the beautiful Harley some more compliments. I particularly liked the star between his eyes with its unusual long lower point that ran like the trail of a comet almost to the tip of his nose.

"And he looks powerful too," I finished. "Do you do a lot of show jumping with him?"

"Mostly cross-country." Daniel leaned forward and patted his horse affectionately. "There aren't many shows to go to on Morvona, although we do sometimes take a trip to the mainland for a competition. My brothers and I have built a pretty good event course near our house. You'll have to bring Gable over and give him a go."

"I'd love to. We haven't done much cross-country but we're entered for an event in September so the practice would be great."

"You can come and try it out now if you like." I'd have happily followed him home right then only my cell phone started ringing and of course it was my dad.

"Hello." I made my voice bright for Dad but tried to sound kind of offhand in case Daniel thought the call was childish. "Oh hi, Dad. No, I'm fine. Yes, I'm at the coast and it's amazing. Well, actually I was going to ring you because I might be a bit later than I said."

Daniel must have heard the quacking noise that was my dad's voice becoming louder with alarm. I raised my eyebrows at him, pulled a comic face to show how cool I was, and tried to calm Dad down.

"No, I told you I'm fine. There's nothing wrong—it's just I met—um—someone who says I can go to his house and practice on a jumping course."

Daniel definitely heard my dad's bellow at that point and I squashed the phone really close to my ear so he wouldn't get the full force of the whole, "You can't go home with some guy you just met. Who is he anyway?" and, "I want you heading for Rockrose now or I'm coming to find you!"

I can usually get my own way with my dad but it can take quite a lot of hard work, and I didn't want Daniel witnessing the show, so I just agreed I'd go straight back and hung up quickly.

"My dad—er—needs me back at the cottage," I said. "So thanks for the invite, but maybe I could come over another day?"

"Okay." He was acting cool as well so I couldn't tell if he was as disappointed as I was. "I'll ride over and see you sometime. Can you find your own way back?"

"No problem." I gave my best upbeat smile to show how unconcerned I was. "I'll see you then."

He nodded, giving a grin that didn't reach his eyes, then turned Harley and cantered away, leaving me with a heart that instead of cartwheeling with joy now felt as though it had sunk like a big heavy stone.

Chapter Three

Sulkily, I turned Gable and started hacking back to the cottage, and not even another extended canter when we left the cliff could lift my mood. I blamed my dad, of course, for treating me like a six-year-old and humiliating me in front of Daniel.

"Now Daniel will never bother coming to see me," I moaned at my pony. "And you and I won't get our cross-country practice and we'll spend the whole holiday plodding around following a mountain bike like a little kid on a lead rein and it's all Dad's fault!"

Gable blew down his nose and jogged a bit, bored with our slow pace (and probably with my whining), but I wouldn't let him canter again, thinking spitefully that I'd make sure we were late home so Dad could worry. He did worry too, and I hadn't even reached the farm before my phone went off and there was Dad's voice, all het-up and anxious.

"Tia! Are you okay? I'm at the top of the hill and I can't see you."

He was actually out looking for me! Treating me like a child or what?

"I'm on my way," I said curtly and heard him expel his breath in relief.

"Good. I should have said to bring your new friend with you; he could have lunch with us."

"Bit late for that," I said bitterly. "He's gone and I probably won't ever see him again."

"Don't be such a drama queen." Dad sounded quite cross. "Of course you will. I'm going back to the cottage so hurry up."

He clicked off irritably but I still wouldn't increase Gable's pace and it was another half an hour before we strolled into Rockrose's garden. I could see from the crease between his eyes that Dad had started fretting again, and I felt a sudden stab of contrition.

"Sorry, Dad." I made a big effort to stop the sulking.

"But you shouldn't have worried. Daniel was really nice and we would have been fine."

"I daresay, but you just can't go off with someone you've never met before."

"So you said." I'd untacked Gable and now I led him back into his field. "But it's not a problem now, is it? He looked ticked off when I said no so I don't think he'll bother asking me again."

"I could look up Creech in the phonebook." Dad was eager to make amends. "I can phone his parents and check them out—"

"Don't you dare!" I was mortified. "Daniel would think I'm about ten years old."

He sighed in frustration, obviously not understanding at all.

"Forget it." I washed my hands under the garden tap. "Let's eat."

He'd made my favorite salad and, while we were having lunch, told me about his morning.

"It wasn't as productive as I'd hoped. The library has several references to the shipwreck in the local section but mentions of the horse were pretty vague. The museum had some handwritten letters, hard to decipher, from local people at the time; they spoke of sightings of the horse but nothing firsthand. Oh, and there was a painting."

I was still feeling sulky inside but managed to respond. "Really? Of the horse? Was he handsome?"

"Couldn't tell. It was a very faded watercolor of the cliff and a raging sea with what could be a swimming horse in the distance."

He was clearly disappointed. I couldn't help feeling our trip to Morvona was getting off to a very shaky start.

"Maybe the people at the farm will know something." I tried to be encouraging. "I said hello on my way out and she seemed friendly."

"They might, I suppose," he said, thinking about it. "If they're an old island family they'll have heard of the legend of course."

"Sure," I said, thinking gloomily that I'd missed the chance of asking Daniel if he knew about the horse. "We could ask when we go and fetch our milk and stuff."

"Good idea." Dad started to look more cheerful. "I—

" He broke off to go indoors as the phone in the cottage started ringing.

I supposed drearily that it was his agent or someone and wondered what to do with the rest of the day. I wanted to do some jumping practice, but after this morning I couldn't see Dad agreeing to let me go very far without him. It would be very easy to sink into a bad mood again but I was trying to be mature, wasn't I, so I plastered on a smile to greet Dad when he came back.

"So you won't be hearing from that young guy again then?" He had a teasing expression on his face.

I looked at him suspiciously. "What d'you mean?"

"That was Mrs. Creech on the phone, Julie her name is. She said Daniel was keen for you to try out the cross-country jumps and would I like to go along too so I can meet them?"

"No!" My face felt as though it was burning. "What did you say? Oh Dad, you didn't tell them you wanted to check them out?"

"No, I didn't. *Julie* suggested I'd probably like to know with whom you intended spending your time."

I thought Daniel's mother sounded nearly as overprotective as my dad, but who cared?—Daniel and I were going to get together and that's what counted.

Julie Creech had given instructions on how to reach Tarag House by road and after our usual disagreement about what time to leave—I wanted *now* and Dad wanted to work a couple of hours first—we reached a compromise and hitched up the trailer an hour or so later. I had wanted to ride Gable there, but Dad insisted we take the trailer and go together, even though it was farther by road. Gable, rested and refreshed, seemed happy to be on the move again. I looked out at the landscape with great interest as we drove carefully along the narrow lanes. The island was definitely wilder at this northern end, and the journey took longer than I thought.

"When I met Daniel on the cliffs he said his house was quite nearby," I remarked. "But these snaky little roads make it seem a lot farther."

"You and Gable probably took the most direct route," Dad agreed. "Looking at the map, Tarag House is only two or three miles toward the coast from Rockrose, but taking the inland route means we're having to drive a lot farther. Look out for a sizable chunk of rock—the turning for the house is just past it, Julie said."

"There!" I pointed ahead where a great lump of rough sandstone towered at the side of the lane. Just beyond it an even narrower track wound its way into the distance. We crawled slowly along it, Gable's trailer rattling and swaying behind us. I'd thought our holiday cottage was remote but Tarag House, when it finally came into view, seemed literally in the middle of nowhere, surrounded on all sides by trees and grass, which in turn faded into rough, untended stretches of waving fescue, wildflowers, and dark woods. The house wasn't particularly big and certainly not grand but it stood on a gently sloping hill, the soft gray of its old stone mellowed and blurred by years of sun, wind, and rain. It looked as though it *belonged* there, as though instead of being built it had grown from the soil of the rugged countryside and was pleased to be there.

"Lovely," Dad said, and I knew he was getting the same feeling.

Daniel had mentioned brothers, so I'd geared myself

up mentally to be ultra-cool when greeted by a bunch of masculine Creeches, but as we drew up on the gravel outside the house just one small woman, one large man, and what looked like twenty dogs were there, waving and smiling. (Well, the dogs were wagging and panting.)

Dad jumped out and held out his hand. "Brett Carberry," he said. "You must be Julie and Tam."

They shook hands and Julie said, "And where's Tia?"

I got out and was immediately surrounded by the dogs (only five of them—not as many as I'd thought). Julie, who looked very kind and smiley, rapidly ran through their names. Just as I was sorting out which was which they all started barking and the tail wagging became so intense I was practically blown over by the wind it made.

"They've heard Daniel," Tam said. We turned to see the stunning black Harley and his rider appear from behind the house.

They cantered easily across to join us and, feeling my face start heating up again, I got very busy with the ramp of the trailer so Daniel wouldn't wonder why I'd suddenly turned into an overripe tomato. He must have been feeling pretty self-conscious too; we just grunted hi, and he slid off Harley to hold Gable while I did up the girth.

"Aren't you two going to have a drink with us before you start riding?" Julie asked. I groaned inwardly at the thought of sitting stiffly round a table making small talk.

My dad, bless him, winked at me and said, "Tia's itching to take a look at this cross-country course of yours. Maybe Daniel could show her round it and we'll all get together later."

"Are you sure you're okay with that, Brett?" Tam looked doubtful. "Our boys are used to it, but it's quite a hefty course so if you're worried about Tia—"

"Dad never worries about my *riding*," I said firmly. They all laughed, guessing, I suppose, just how much he worried about everything else.

They, and four of the dogs, made their way into the house. I breathed a sigh of relief at being left with just the horses, Daniel, and a very hairy hound called Finn.

"You don't mind showing me round, do you?" I'd stopped blushing so was able to smile and look at him directly.

"No, it's good. I can't stand all that question-and-answer stuff the parents go in for. Could be worse, though. If my brothers had been here they'd be giving me a hard time."

"Where are they all?" I pulled down my stirrup irons and hopped into Gable's saddle.

"There are only two. Twins, Ben and Marcus. They're spending the summer on a ranch in Argentina, pretending to be gauchos."

"Fantastic!" I was envious. "Are they going to be cowboys as a career?"

He laughed, showing white teeth that looked great against his tan. "No, they're both hoping to be vets. South America's a sort of pre-college adventure."

"Brilliant, I'd love to do that. Or maybe jump racing in Ireland or trekking in the Spanish mountains."

"Quite the adventurous sort then, Tia?" He gave the fabulous grin again. "In which case you're definitely going to like our little jumping course!"

He turned Harley and led the way, walking briskly to warm the two horses up while Finn loped alongside. The grounds adjacent to the old house were well tended and lovely, but soon we were moving across rougher grass that swept into a wooded valley below.

"I'll walk you through first," Daniel said. "Gable can have a good look at all the jumps and you can decide which ones you want to try."

"All of them, obviously," I said. He raised his eyebrows and gave a wolfish grin.

"Wait till you see them before you decide."

I shrugged, thinking nothing was going to make me change my mind, and followed Harley and Finn into the dappled shade of the wood. The first jump was just ahead, a solid construction of heavy planks built around a thick, prickly hedge. It was both high and wide but I knew, given a good approach, Gable would have no problem. My confidence, always pretty high when it came to riding, rose farther and slightly cockily. Fence number two was an old wagon, filled with earth and planted with shrubs, and I saw Gable's ears flick when he saw it. Still, I thought, not too bad, and followed Harley's shining rump and Finn's hairy one round the rest of the course.

Well, what can I say? Scary? Terrifying? *Absolutely!*

There were twenty fences in all, ranging from natural (huge) obstacles like fallen trees and ditches to ingenious articles like a massive rough-built table, a mighty pyramid of tractor tires, and a cute-looking, but hard-to-jump, brick building complete with red-tiled roof that Daniel said was a disused duck house. A fast-flowing stream ran through the copse and they'd cleverly wound the course around it so you jumped over it from one angle; from another you jumped into it and out of it; and at its widest point you cleared solid rails to jump into the water, then splashed across, and leapt over an upturned boat to get out! Daniel showed us every fence but offered no advice or comment until we reached the end. Then he sat back in his saddle and grinned at me again.

"So, what d'you think, Tia?"

I cleared my throat. "Impressive." I wanted to sound cool but my voice came out very squeaky. I saw the devilish grin widen.

"We think so. D'you want to get warmed up and have a go?"

Did he mean the whole course? He had to be joking—

I'd never *seen* anything like it, let alone ridden it! I swallowed several times and hoped my voice would sound more normal.

"OKAY."

He laughed out loud then, throwing back his head and showing more white teeth. "Whew! You're either incredibly brave or very, very dumb, Tia Carberry. And I'd say you're actually pretty bright so how about just trying him over the first fence and maybe the plain one into the water?"

Relief flooded through me, but I managed merely to nod nonchalantly. "If you like."

We did some proper warming up, then went back into the copse. We concentrated on the simplest jumps, including a very large log. Gable and I enjoyed ourselves so much we didn't want to stop and Daniel was—well, just terrific. We seemed to click straightaway. Not only was he helpful and patient with the jumping, he really seemed to enjoy us being there and it felt as though we'd known each other forever. When we went back to the house we found his parents and my dad seated on a terrace overlooking the valley below.

"We saw you cantering through the trees," Dad greeted me. "You looked great!"

He too looked very happy, and when I discovered Tam Creech had offered to let him nose through the old local history books in his collection, I could see why. It was the start of a magical few days. Every morning I rode with Daniel, sometimes to the coast and cliffs where we first met, and every afternoon he helped us practice our cross-country skills on the Tarag House course. Each time, Daniel introduced another obstacle into our course. I had begun leaving Gable at the Creech farm overnight, turned out with Harley and a couple of sweet older geldings. It meant I went back to Rockrose with Dad in the car, and of course we returned together each morning, giving us plenty of time to chat. Dad spent his days researching in the study, and he and I were in our respective heavens. We would have liked the routine to continue for the whole of our stay but three days later everything was to change when we were suddenly thrown into a strange and disturbing situation that threatened our very presence on the Island of Morvona.

Chapter Four

We knew things were going to change at Tarag House, of course. In the few days we'd known them, the Creech family seemed to have taken to Dad and me pretty strongly, and we'd learned a lot about their life in Morvona. They were an island family, and Tam was able trace his roots several generations back to around 1800 when his great-great-grandfather (or maybe more greats) built Tarag House. Now they were quite big landowners, with several houses and holiday homes (Rockrose being one) and an active participation in encouraging people to visit the remote island. A major hands-on part of this was when several times a year various groups rented the guest wing Tam had created from an old stable block near the main house. In the stone building he'd made six bedrooms with their own bathrooms, a big communal hall, and a well-equipped kitchen. Sometimes, if the group was large, like a Pony Club or Scout troop, a tented camp was also erected, Daniel told me, but just six older students were expected this time.

"They're studying botany and geology at a university in Wales," he explained. "Morvona's got several rare plant forms and some of them grow practically out of the bare rock of our cliffs, so it's interesting scientifically."

"Oh." I couldn't see the attraction, personally. "So will these six guys be all studious and boring?"

"Nah, students are usually a laugh. I have to show them round Morvona a bit, it's part of the package they get when they rent here, and they're usually good fun."

"I could help," I offered. "With the guided tours I mean."

"Thanks, Tia." Daniel was too kind to point out I hardly knew my *own* way around yet. "There'll still be plenty of time for riding and we—" He stopped and listened. "I think I hear the minibus arriving. Come and welcome them in."

We joined Julie as Tam parked by the front door and

went forward to help with the luggage. There were three young guys, aged around twenty or so, and two girls of about the same age.

"Only five?" Julie was busy shaking hands.

"Yeah. Georgia's missed her connection but she phoned to say she'd be on a later ferry," a tall freckly one, who'd introduced himself as Ade, said apologetically. "I think she'll get a taxi from the port. I hope her being late doesn't mess you up."

"It's fine." Julie was in her element, fussing round everyone. "If she's here in time for lunch I've made lots of salad stuff so that'll keep, but a taxi will cost her a fortune. Should Tam go back and pick her up, d'you think?"

"Georgia's got plenty of money." Carrie, a petite brunette, smiled back at her. "It's her own fault she's late. She's always doing a million things at once."

My dad had picked up Carrie's big duffel while Daniel, I noticed from the corner of my eye, was walking easily with the smaller bag belonging to a tall, stunning redhead called Sara. Dominic and Jeff, one fairish and jokey, the other dark and serious, carried their own stuff and followed Tam into the Old Stables, ducking their heads as they went through the low front door.

"Wow, nice." They all seemed to like the lovely rooms Tam had made and were soon tucking into Julie's food and chatting away with us all in a really easy, friendly way.

I'd been a bit concerned at having all these strangers descend upon Tarag House but it seemed fine, especially as Daniel, once he'd deposited the luggage, had left the beautiful Sara and come straight back to join me. Once lunch was over we showed the students around the place, then left them to settle and chill out while Daniel and I took the horses for more cross-country practice, Tam went back to his gardening, Julie walked the dogs, and Dad headed straight for the study and his beloved old books. Our riding session in the copse went pretty well but I was surprised at how spooked my pony still was by some of the jumps.

"I've never had any trouble with show jumping," I told Daniel. "Even the first time we tried colored poles Gable was fine. He's totally laid-back as a rule."

"Yeah, I can see that, he's doing great really. Some

horses go nuts when you show them something weird like a duck house or an old boat, whereas Gable's just a bit hesitant. He needs to get his confidence from you."

I knew he was right and if I'm honest some of the massive fences scared me a bit, so I suppose it's no wonder poor Gable wasn't a hundred percent sure. Still, this was the point of practicing. Daniel made sure we never overfaced him or made the session too long, and we always ended with a jump he liked so I could revel in the joyous way Gable powered toward it and soared over, his natural athleticism combining with the training he was enjoying. And with all the hard work we were doing, I was positive my pony and I would just fly the course in that September competition.

Dad was as enthusiastic as me about the setup. He'd found some barely legible diaries from the Creech family of a hundred and fifty years ago and was having a wonderful time deciphering them, in between expeditions to the woods, cliffs, and beaches he'd found mentioned.

"The journals are written by one of the Creech sons and they give an invaluable insight into the day-to-day life back then," he'd told me excitedly the day before.

"But is there any mention of the shipwreck and the horse?" I asked in reply. "That's what you're hoping to find, isn't it?"

"Nothing yet but I'm hoping that's to come. The ink in the diaries is very faded and young Ben, the writer, only put the day and month, not the year, so I don't know the exact date at present."

"Ben Creech? One of Daniel's brothers is called that. Is the olden-days Ben a twin as well?"

"D'you know, he might be." Dad, driving carefully along the winding road, looked thoughtful. "He keeps mentioning a Tam who seems to be around his own age."

"Cool!" I liked the idea of family names being handed down the generations. "Maybe you'll find a journal by this Tam as well."

His eyes had sparkled and he'd grabbed the first opportunity he could to get back to the study. Now, as Daniel and I returned from the horses' field where Gable and Harley were enjoying a rest, I tapped gently on the study window as we passed.

LEGEND OF THE ISLAND HORSE

"Come on, Dad—we're going to see if the students want anything."

"Oh leave him." Daniel peered in to look at all the books and papers spread over the big desk. "It's okay, Brett, we'll sort it, you don't have to come along."

"He volunteered to help," I pointed out. "He said it's the least we can do when your family has made us so welcome."

"You don't have to repay us, we like you guys being around," Daniel said. I felt a surge of the lovely warm glow I was experiencing a lot these days.

I'd have preferred life to stay as it was, but, like Dad said, it was just good manners to help the Creeches any way we could with their visitors. I must say it was a relief to know the students seemed a nice group and very laidback too. They were quite happy to lounge around talking and joking with us and didn't require any energetic guided tours at present.

"We'll wait till Georgia gets here for all that," Ade said. "She's the live wire, always got to be doing something."

"And she'll be mad as hell if we get to see something she

doesn't," Dominic, the cheerful, fair one of the guys, said with a laugh. "Georgia likes to be first in everything."

The others smiled philosophically but I saw Sara raise her beautiful eyebrows as though she was less than keen on the thought of the yet-to-arrive student. It was a gorgeous summer's day so they'd taken a tray of cold drinks out to the garden and were lolling on the comfortable old wicker chairs or lying on the grass.

"Tam pointed out the cross-country course where you two were practicing." Ade rolled over and looked up at Daniel and me. "We were going to come down and watch but Carrie's scared of horses."

"No need to be afraid." Daniel smiled at the petite brunette. "There's no way they'd hurt you."

"It's not that, I'm just a complete sap about them." She looked embarrassed. "But I told the others to go—Tam said you were both worth watching."

"Daniel's great." I felt really sorry for her being too frightened to even come near a horse. "But I'm still pretty rubbish."

"You are so *not*," Daniel said immediately. I was really

glad he looked at me in a completely different way than when he talked to Carrie or even the beautiful Sara.

It was very pleasant in the lovely, peaceful garden so when a taxi came screeching to a halt a few yards away and a very loud, carrying voice could be heard arguing with the driver, we all sat up and turned our heads toward the noise.

"Oh hooray, it's Georgia," Sara said sardonically. The dark, quiet one called Jeff nudged her.

"It's all right, don't let her wind you up," he said.

I was beginning to feel nervous about meeting the last one of the six to arrive, as I'd started to imagine someone large and terrifying, so when a tiny, beautifully dressed blond girl bounced across to join us, I was quite taken aback.

"Hi you guys. Here I am at last! What a klutz missing you at the ferry—how you all doing?" She then rushed up and hugged everyone, chatting nonstop. "Carrie, honey, I love your hair—who did it? Jeff, how was your beach holiday, phew what a tan! Ade, baby, more freckles!"

It was a bit like being hit by a small but very forceful

tornado, and Daniel and I blinked and stepped back in-stinctively. Once she'd finished greeting, cuddling, and yelling at all her friends, she spotted us.

"Oh cute! I didn't know there were going to be kids here! And so good looking too! Aren't you just darling?"

She made a grab for me but, being several inches shorter, only managed to plant a kiss on my chin. I saw Daniel draw himself up his full six feet so she could only air-kiss around shoulder height. Tam and Julie, having heard the taxi, ar-rived in time to deflect her enthusiasm and she followed them into the Old Stables, still talking at full pitch.

"She does calm down a bit." Ade laughed at our stunned expressions. "But not much."

"Right," Daniel said. "Um—we'd better go and check on the horses, right, Tia?"

Realizing he was trying to escape I grinned and nod-ded, but then Julie called out for us all to go inside. We were going to sneak off anyway, but she spotted us and hustled us in.

"Georgia wants her dinner now," she whispered, look-ing slightly harassed. "So I might as well feed everyone.

Give me a hand you two, will you?"

We followed her into the kitchen, which was an open-plan arrangement off the main room. The group of six were already seated at the dining table, talking (well, mostly listening to Georgia), and we could hear their conversation as we peeled and chopped vegetables. Georgia had spent some of her vacation in London, it appeared, and was telling the others about the amount of designer labels she'd bought.

"And more shoes. Manolo Blahnik, Jimmy Choo, you name it—I got it!"

Sara didn't seem too impressed, but little Carrie was admiring a lot of the things Georgia was holding up.

"I love that blue hooded top. It would look great with my cropped pants."

"Sure you like it—it's the finest cashmere!" Georgia pulled it away from her outstretched hand. "Hey, what's that ring you're wearing, Carrie?"

"I got it in a junk store last week. Cool, isn't it?"

"I told her to get it checked. It looks really old and might be valuable," Sara said.

"Let's see." Georgia's voice was confident. "No way, it's just a cheap copy. I know about this stuff, remember, with my dad being *the* eminent archaeologist. He digs up the real thing all the time."

"Here we go!" Jeff came into the kitchen and slammed down his glass. "Ten minutes here and we've already had the 'I'm so rich and my dad's so famous' bit."

Dominic had followed and put a restraining hand on his arm. "Shut up, Jeff. It's just Georgia's way—no big deal."

"Yeah, but she should think before she mouths off. Did you see Sara's face when she was showing all that designer crap? While Georgia was in London spending like money was going out of fashion, Sara was working her butt off waitressing so she could afford this trip."

"All right, all right." Dominic sighed and glanced round as we self-consciously carried on working. "Come on, Jeff, we shouldn't be bothering these nice folks."

They went back to the other room, switched on the big TV, and started shouting the answers to some quiz show or other, obviously intending to drown out Georgia's endless prattle. Because of the racket I didn't hear my dad enter; it wasn't until I heard the note of excitement in his voice that I realized he was calling me.

"Hiyah, Dad." Wiping my hands, I went in to see him.

His eyes were glittering and his hands were slightly shaky but he very politely greeted Georgia when she was introduced.

"Sorry, sorry, I'm interrupting you all—I just wanted to tell Tia about the horse."

"Horse? Hey, you guys have horses? I *love* horses!" The blond girl prepared to go off in full spate again but Daniel had joined us and he explained very briefly who we were and what my dad was doing.

Before Georgia could say *Research? I love research!* I quickly asked him what he'd found.

"A definite sighting of the horse!"

"No!" I was genuinely thrilled. "A firsthand account— it's just what you were hoping for."

His face fell, but only slightly. "It's not exactly that. Ben writes that his brother, Tam, has seen the horse from the shipwreck. But—and this is the exciting bit—two months later his journal states that not only has Tam seen the horse again—he's actually sketched it and intends to produce a painting!"

"Fantastic." I gave him a quick hug and looked round at the others. "It's a real breakthrough, and if Dad could find the horse's picture—"

"We'll help!" Georgia, who couldn't possibly have taken in the whole story, was immediate enthusiasm. "Won't we, you guys? This looks a great old building and we can all help you search it—er—Jet."

"Brett, my name's Brett," he corrected her absently. "It's very kind of you but I wouldn't dream of encroaching on your study module. You all start your own research tomorrow, don't you?"

"Yeah, yeah, but we'll find time for your legend horse thing as well." Georgia was undeniably irritating, but you had to admire her energy.

Dad's entrance had managed to divert attention from her, thank goodness, and we all ate Julie's excellent meal together, amicably discussing the legend and the history of the island without the blond girl taking center stage. In fact, after her initial storming arrival, she did seem to have quieted down a lot. Apart from making a big fuss later about wanting to wash and blow-dry Carrie's hair because, as she said, "The new cut is so cute but it needs some lift and movement in it, sweetie!" she actually lapsed into a thoughtful near-silence.

This seemed to suit the three guys, who got more and more raucous in a funny, slapstick kind of way, and Daniel and I thoroughly enjoyed our evening with them all. Dad was over at the house with Julie and Tam and it was quite late before we left, but I promised Daniel we'd be back early the following morning.

"That'll be great." His dark eyes looked warmly into mine. "Dad's driving the students to Barrow Bay and they're heading off along the cliff path. I'm to meet them around twelve and guide them back cross-country. I'd kinda like you to come too."

"Okay," I said, real casual. "I guess I'd better come along and help you in case things turn ugly between them!"

It was a silly, throwaway joke, of course, and I had no way of knowing how very close to the truth it would turn out to be.

Chapter Five

It was obvious from the moment we arrived next morning that there was trouble. Tam had parked the minibus out front and Carrie, Jeff, and Dominic were already sitting inside, but we could hear voices coming from the Old Stables that were very loud and clearly quarreling.

"I don't care what you were looking for, Georgia." Sara came stomping out, her red hair glowing like a beacon. "You don't just walk in and start nosing through my stuff, got it?"

"Sara, she has tried to explain." Peacemaker Ade followed, putting out a hand to hold her arm. She shook him off furiously.

"Load of baloney. If she wants to hunt for Brett's legend picture that's fine, but she should check with people first."

"For God's sake." Georgia, in another fabulous outfit, strolled out behind them. "It's not like you've got anything valuable. Why so touchy? I had a look round Carrie's room and she didn't throw a tantrum."

"Oh Lord!" My dad groaned quietly and moved quickly forward. "Georgia, it's kind of you to help but I really don't want you upsetting your friends like this. Sara, I'm really sorry—"

"I don't blame *you*." The tall girl stamped aboard the bus and threw her rucksack on a seat at the back.

"I'll try and calm her down," Ade muttered. "Georgia, you better stay with Carrie."

"Jeez." Georgia puffed out her cheeks and looked at us. "What a fuss over nothing! It's not like I sent one of the guys to hunt in Sara's room. Though maybe that's where I went wrong—I guess she'd have liked that."

"Don't be more of a bitch than you have to." Jeff leaned out and grabbed her smart bag. "And hurry up. You've held us up long enough."

Georgia shrugged and climbed aboard, turning to smile at us. "Seems I'm not exactly flavor of the month. But don't worry, Brett, I'll still help with your legend horse."

"I really wish she wouldn't," Dad said with another groan as we watched Tam drive the six students away.

I noticed Jeff had gone to sit with Sara and was talking earnestly to her, his dark head very close to hers. Ade was keeping Georgia as far away as possible while little Carrie gazed out the window as if determined to find the scenery much more interesting than the feud going on around her.

"I thought it was going to be good fun having them here," I said slightly bitterly. "They were great yesterday but since Georgia arrived it's all changed."

"She's a bit over the top," Dad agreed. "But I feel guilty letting my enthusiasm for the legend run away with me and infecting her with it. It didn't occur to me she'd start hunting straightaway."

"And in the Old Stables too! Tam must have torn the place apart when he converted it. What was the sense in Georgia poking around in there?"

"Don't ask me, I'm still reeling at Sara's reaction!" My poor dad's not great with displays of female emotion.

"Oh well, let's hope they've all simmered down by the

time Daniel and I meet up with them. Where is he anyway?"

"I'm right here." Daniel appeared, grinning. "I brought Gable and Harley in and gave them a brush-down," he went on. "Your boy's been rolling so it took a while."

"He likes to find the dirtiest patch." I laughed and walked with him to the yard where our horses were waiting.

Dad, of course, went straight to the house and the hundred-and-fifty-year-old journal of Ben Creech.

"Did you hear the spat between Sara and Georgia?" I asked Daniel as we carried our saddles from the tack room.

"No? What was their problem?"

I told him how mad the red-haired girl had got and about my dad feeling responsible for Georgia's involvement.

"It's not his fault," Daniel said loyally. "That girl's a liability—a real fruitcake. I agree with her about one thing, though—it sounds like something out of nothing so I'm sure they'll all be over it by the time we meet up."

"Barrow Bay you said we're going, didn't you? Is it a

good ride?"

"A bit wild in places." He swung easily into the saddle. "So I guess in your book, Miss Tia-Knows-No-Fear, it's a pretty good ride."

I hopped aboard Gable and pretended to jab Daniel with my riding crop for being cheeky. Laughing, we left the yard and headed west for the coast. I was beginning to know this route with its mixture of narrow stony trails, broad gallops, and dark patches of dense woodland. The first stretch of open turf came after twenty minutes or so. We'd walked a good way, then trotted, so the horses were well warmed up and they both began to prance and rock when they felt their hooves touch the springy grass beneath them. Open countryside spread before us, perfect for a gallop, and as soon as I shifted my weight and took up the forward position Gable was off, the sheer joy of speed lengthening his stride. He was leading with his right and I could feel the four-time sequence—left hind, right hind, left fore, right fore—blending and soaring into an exhilarating sense of flight. I was still in control, of course, Gable continuing to accept the bit as I urged him forward, feeling rather than seeing the rapidly approaching presence of Harley. I could hear them clearly, the pounding of the black horse's hooves and the deep chuckle from Daniel as the two of them gained ground. Now they were beside us, Harley stretching his neck like a racehorse, Daniel crouching, beautifully balanced, in the saddle as they prepared to go past.

But Gable and I weren't finished and I gave the aid for increased impulsion, feeling the added swell of power as he surged forward to stay ahead. Daniel laughed out loud then and came back at us, Harley's fine black head with its trailing star racing cheek-by-cheek with Gable's gleaming bay. We galloped, locked together, along the length of the gently undulating track till eventually the broad turf climbed steeply uphill and we pulled up together to stand, breathless and ecstatic, at the edge of a wood.

"Wow!" Daniel's dark eyes were shining. "You two are *good*."

I shook back the long hair that flowed from under my helmet. "Thought you'd beat us, huh? We're tougher than we look!"

"You look—you look—" He didn't seem able to find the right word. "And yeah, Gable's faster than I thought. On the flat anyway."

"Just wait till we get the hang of all those jumps," I teased him. "Then maybe you won't be able to catch us at cross-country either."

"No chance." He was back to his usual jokey self, but his eyes still held that gleam of stunned admiration. "Come on then."

We walked the two horses into the shady depths of the wood, perfect for cooling them down as they stretched their necks on a long rein. Their hooves made very little sound on the thick covering of old leaves. A gentle breeze stirred the green-gold canopy above us, causing the trees to sway and whisper. It took fifteen minutes or so to traverse the wood, and when we emerged at the other end we both blinked as the unaccustomed rays of the sun dazzled our eyes. We were now on a rough, stony track leading to the clifftop. I leaned forward eagerly, anticipating the stunning view as we crested the hill.

And there it was, a glorious panoramic vista of the

ocean, stretching to infinity, its depths reflecting the clear azure blue of the sky. We cantered across the scrubby vegetation on the clifftop, then reined the horses in and sat looking out to sea while way, way beneath us its waves lapped and pounded against the jagged rocks of the cliff base. It was too beautiful for words and I was glad that Daniel only smiled at my ecstatic face, sharing but not spoiling the moment. We'd only ever ridden this far before, turning inland to take a different route back to Tarag House, but today we followed the faint track that led along the cliff edge, walking with the sea at our right shoulder.

"How long before we reach Barrow Bay?" I asked Daniel, having lost all sense of time.

He glanced at his watch. "It's about twenty minutes from here, but we don't have to be there till noon. I've got a surprise for you first."

I'm always up for something new so I looked round with interest, wondering whether he was planning to turn inland and maybe try jumping something strange and enormous. Instead, with left leg and right rein, he guided

Harley toward the very edge of the cliff, and for one heart-stopping moment I thought I was going to watch them tumble over the side.

"Come on." He turned in his saddle and gave me that grin. "We're going for a paddle!"

I gulped and followed, leaning back in my seat as Gable's neat hooves picked our way carefully between a line of boulders marking a twisting track down the side of the cliff. Without even a hint of a stumble my clever pony reached the fine, dark gold sand of the bay and trotted eagerly forward to join Harley as he stood hock-deep in the ocean. The sea lapped lazily around us, making that lovely murmuring sound of summer, as Gable lowered his head and blew at it curiously. Harley snorted and held up a foreleg, splashing down hard in the foam.

"Is he telling Gable not to drink it?" I laughed.

"No, I think he's saying, 'Let's gallop through it'—it's what he likes best," Daniel said, grinning back at me. "Let Gable get used to it first, though—this is his first time in the ocean, isn't it?"

"Yeah." I rode my pony a little deeper into the gentle

waves. "There's a river at home but it's not very deep. We just ride across it occasionally. I think he's really enjoying this, though."

It was true, Gable seemed to love the feel of the moving water. We splashed around for a while longer while Harley pranced and swayed like a rocking horse in his eagerness to be off. The bay wasn't big but the cliffs around it curved in a perfect arc, making the stretch of sand at the water's edge quite long and very inviting. All the beaches I've ever visited have been packed with sunbathers and swimmers, kids playing in the sand and people with ice cream, inflatable boats, and Jet Skis—you know the kind of scene—but here on Morvona we shared the whole stunning bay with just a few seagulls and unseen marine life. Daniel told me nearly all the beaches at the northern end of the island were like this.

"It's because they're so hard to reach," he explained. "There are no roads nearby so you have to either trek for miles and then clamber down a steep cliff or come in by boat, which is dangerous because of all the rocks offshore."

Just like in the shipwreck Dad was researching, I

thought. "Is this where the legend began then? Are we where the Island Horse swam ashore?"

"No, that's farther north again—it's called North Bay, in fact, and it's really, *really* wild and remote. This one is Coral Cove and it's one of my favorites. Listen, Tia, if you think Gable's okay I think we should have a gallop before Harley pulls my arms out."

"All right."

Cheekily I nipped past him at canter, and at the lightest touch Gable soared into gallop, his flying hooves kicking up spray that spun around us in a million diamond droplets. I heard Daniel laugh and then Harley was racing too, splashing and thundering through the shallow, glittering waves. It was fabulous, mind-blowing fun and I could have gone on forever. As we approached the sweep of cliffs that formed the headland, Daniel, racing alongside now, began giving half-halts and we slowed through canter into walk then halt, the horses breathing deeply as they stood up to their knees in water.

"You seemed to take to that pretty well!" He grinned at me. "I can't get used to having a horse around who can match Harley for speed. Ben and Marcus have Appaloosas, great horses, but they can't get near him."

"Gable's amazing," I agreed, lying forward and hugging my clever pony's neck. "He can do anything."

"What's he like with swimming? We can leave their stuff on those rocks and take them in for a real dip."

The answer was I had no idea; we'd never been anywhere to try. Fired up with enthusiasm, I had my pony unsaddled and my boots and half chaps off. Daniel took everything off except some baggy swim trunks and I was very pleased to note he was extremely fit. I was stuck with my riding pants, but I was grateful for them too, feeling self-conscious and giddy at the same time. In fact as we walked the horses deeper and deeper into the sea, the combination of the half-naked Daniel and the gleaming ebony Harley was quite overpowering; I had to concentrate hard not to go all wobbly. But then Gable was swimming and I forgot everything else; it was all so new and fantastic. My pony loved it too, seeming to feel no fear, just striking out strongly and forging swiftly through the deep blue water. Daniel called out not to tire him by going too far, though, so reluctantly we turned and headed back for the shore.

"He did brilliantly and we'll stay in longer next time. Anyhow we have to get them dry and go off to Barrow Bay, remember."

"Oh heck, we're meeting up with the students from hell," I pretended to grumble. "Let's hope Georgia and Sara have finished their catfight. What are we supposed to do with them anyway?"

"We show them how to get down the cliff so they can picnic on the beach." Daniel had the day's instructions off by heart. "Then after lunch I take them to a place called Barrow Wood where some rare orchids grow. They've got a map obviously but the orchid clearing is really hard to find so we've always supplied botany groups with a guide."

It was now late morning and the sun, high in a clear blue sky, was pretty hot so it didn't take long for us all to dry. We led the horses along the beach so the warm breeze would help, then got dressed and saddled up to head off for our meeting with the students. We were joining them on the clifftop a mile or so farther along, and as we got nearer I could see they were already there and waiting. We both waved cheerfully and I was glad to see all of them waved in return. I hoped this meant they were all happy and we weren't going to have our lovely day spoiled. But all I can say is—I was wrong!

Chapter Six

Difficulties began straightaway. As soon as reached the group Carrie squeaked and dived behind Ade, and we remembered the horse phobia she'd talked about.

"Ah." Daniel looked slightly nonplussed. "It's a tricky kind of trail leading down to the beach so we were going to take your backpacks and lead the way. Will that be okay with you, Carrie?"

"Sure, Daniel." She peeped out timidly at him. "I'll just stay as far away from the ponies as possible if you don't mind."

"That's fine." He dismounted and handed Harley's reins to me. "Let's have your bags, then, and I'll rope them together."

He was very quick and efficient, looping the rope over Harley's back so two backpacks hung either side of the saddle. I took the other two and placed one on each side in front of me, hoping my good-tempered pony wouldn't mind acting as packhorse. We then led the way down a zigzagging route to reach the bottom of the cliff and another lovely sandy cove. The students followed us, scrabbling and using their hands on steep parts, with Carrie the last in line. There was quite a lot of laughing and mild swearing from the guys and girlie squeals from Sara and Carrie but they all agreed it was worth the effort once they were standing by the sea as it lapped invitingly on the shore.

"Fantastic! I *love* the ocean. Come on, everyone—swim first, eat later." Georgia seemed back to her finest loudest form and was already scrabbling about in her backpack.

"Hang on." Daniel jumped down to the sand and quickly undid the ropes, so I slid off Gable and did the same. "Okay, everyone, here are your bags. This is a great place for a swim—just stay within the bay where it's completely safe and we'll see you in a couple of hours."

"Oh, aren't you kids staying for a picnic too?" Georgia had stripped down to a gorgeous bikini and was tying her hair back with a matching colored band.

"No, we're taking the horses inland a short way so they can have a rest and some shade."

As he spoke I saw Carrie's shoulders relax immediately.

"But we'll be back to show you the orchid trail," Daniel added, straightening his own backpack before he remounted.

They all said thanks as they rushed to change into swimming gear. We very nearly made it off the beach before the trouble began. As usual it was Georgia who sparked it.

"Hey, don't forget to take off your jewelry." She was removing a gold ankle bracelet. "I lost a diamond earring on a beach in the South of France last year."

I heard Sara sigh theatrically but Ade and Dominic took off their wristwatches and handed them to Georgia, who put them carefully in her bag.

"Come on, girls," she trilled bossily. As I rode past Sara I saw her take out the silver hoops she wore in her ears.

Jeff took them from her and went to hand them over, but Carrie was already walking toward the sea edge and hadn't responded.

"Carrie—you haven't taken off your ring," Georgia yelled.

The small, dark girl kept going, obviously keen to get away from Gable and Harley. "It's really tight," she called. "It won't come off."

"It'll probably fall off once you're wet." Georgia wouldn't let it go. "Stop being a crybaby about these horses and come back here."

"Leave her alone," Sara growled immediately. "She's not being a wimp; she's got a real phobia."

"Mind your own business, I'm just trying to help her," Georgia snapped back without even looking at her. "Carrie! Carrie—"

"Oh give it a rest. She doesn't care if she loses the thing anyway." Jeff dumped Sara's earrings into Georgia's hand. "It's not like it's worth anything."

Georgia held up the silver hoops and sneered. "Unlike these pieces of priceless junk!"

"Shut up, you cow!" Sara, who'd started following Carrie, turned furiously. "You're still bitching because we don't want to play your stupid hunt-the-legend game. I came here to get study points, not to help you chat up some nutty author."

"Hey!" I wanted to leave but I wasn't having that. "Don't you start on my dad! He doesn't even want you lot joining in his project."

"Oh butt out, kid. Georgia enjoys fighting her own battles." Jeff had it all wrong, and Daniel leapt in straightaway.

"If you listened," he said hotly, "you'd find Tia's defending her *father*. And could you all stop calling us kids—it's not us who need to grow up!"

"Okay, okay." Ade held up his hands. "Let's go in and have a nice cooling-off swim, guys. Thanks for bringing us down here, Daniel and Tia, and sorry if the bad temper's ricocheting in your direction. We'll see you later, yeah?"

Still feeling huffy, I nodded and moved as quickly as I could back up the twisting cliff path, followed by Daniel and Harley.

"Huh!" I was surprised at how mad I felt. "Saying that about my dad!"

"You mean you've never heard him called a nutty author?" Daniel tried to keep it light. "I thought all writers were a bit loopy. It's part of the charm."

"Not that. I meant about Georgia chatting him up. You don't think she fancies him, do you?"

"I think she likes to be the center of attraction and thinks following up the legend will keep her in the spotlight," Daniel said firmly. "All the others just want to have a laugh and get on with their studying so they're letting her attention-seeking get to them."

"Hmm." I wasn't sure. I'd found the interest Georgia had shown in Dad's work quite strange and really, *really* didn't want it to be because she was attracted to him. "It's not that I don't want him to have a girlfriend—he's dated a few times and I'm fine with that—but I wouldn't want one who's a maniac and a lot nearer my age than his!"

"I get you. I wouldn't be keen on Georgia as a potential stepmother either." Daniel gave an elaborate shudder. "Don't worry—a lot of people are fascinated by the legend and I think she's just one of them. A very loud and irritating one, that's all."

"I hope you're right." We were walking the horses toward some trees as their tails swished in the heat of the noonday sun. "You don't say much about the legend. Don't you think it's true?"

"Yeah I do, actually," he said, quite surprising me. "I mean, I know there's no real proof and some say it's just been romanticized over the years, but it's perfectly possible. I think some of the present-day horses on Morvona bear it out anyway."

"How d'you mean?"

"Well, there's been no real program of breeding, but occasionally a local mare will produce a foal of real quality that could be a throwback to some extra-special stallion."

"Who says the horse from the shipwreck was a classy one?" I hadn't heard this.

"No one, in those exact words, but the ship that sank was carrying 'five brood mares and one fine Thoroughbred stallion' that were being transported to a stud farm in Ireland. The country produces the very best National Hunt racehorses so it stands to reason the breeder would have ordered a really good stallion to boost his stock."

I didn't know about this, having not exactly paid a hundred percent attention when Dad was going on about his research. We had nearly reached the shade of the trees, and as I looked at Harley's gleaming black lines a thought struck me.

"Harley! Is he a Morvona horse? One of the unexpectedly gorgeous foals?"

"That's a perfect description." Daniel leaned forward and patted his horse's neck affectionately. "He's from one of my uncle Peter's mares. She's a really nice horse herself, but she'd only ever produced ordinary foals before. Peter was so impressed at Harley he called my parents over to see him and they bought him for me straightaway. That was six years ago when I was ten and I've seen him every day since, even before he came to live with us."

"Lucky you!" I was envious; I'd have loved to know Gable when he was a baby. "Oh, is this where we're going to eat?"

He led the way to a shady clearing in the small wood. A stream gurgled gently and the sun filtered coolly through the dappled shade.

We untacked the horses, slipping on halters so they could drink their fill of the clear water, then sat with our backs against a tree trunk and let them nibble at the short, sweet grass.

"How nice is this?" I looked around and sighed contentedly. "Much better than a hot beach and all those hot tempers."

"Forget 'em." Daniel produced some sandwiches and fruit from his backpack. "I bet you're hungry."

It was great, sitting in the cool shade with Gable's lead rope in one hand and a can of drink in the other. Daniel told me he'd originally planned to rest the horses for an hour and then go back and join the students on the beach.

"But what with all the bickering and sniping, plus Carrie going green every time she looks at Gable and Harley, I've changed my mind. We'll just mooch round here and meet them at the clifftop around two o'clock. Is that okay with you?"

I was totally in favor of the new plan. "Do we have to hang around that orchid place we're showing them?"

"No, we just get them there, then they stay and take photographs and make notes and sketches. It's a hidden kind of spot but once they've been shown where, it's dead easy for them to find the trail back to the main road where my dad will pick them up."

"It's a lot of running around for you all, having them here." I privately thought it a real drag.

"Yeah, but their university was the first college to send a study group to us, so my parents feel a certain obligation. It was a risk setting up the Old Stables because Morvona's not really on the tourist trail. It's too remote, and although it's beautiful it's not easy to get around—as you saw today when we rode down the cliffs."

"So the idea was to encourage people interested in the island itself rather than holidaymakers wanting to flop around on a beach?"

"Yeah, we thought we'd only get students, but we're getting more and more families and groups of friends who just want to rent the Old Stables and have a good time exploring Morvona on their own. They do their own catering and everything, so it's a much easier option for Mum and Dad."

"And for you." I thought he was really good to give up holiday time to act as nursemaid for spoiled students and said so.

"They're not usually any trouble, but then again there's never been a Georgia among them before."

"She is *such* a pain." I was still worrying about her chasing after my dad. "I can see why Sara gets so wound up. Georgia never misses a chance to get at her because Sara hasn't got nice clothes and stuff."

"Hasn't she? I hadn't noticed."

I looked at him. "You're probably too busy ogling her lovely long legs, that's why."

"I hadn't noticed them either." He put his hand on his heart and gave a cheeky grin.

I threw my empty can at him but secretly felt a nice fat glow of satisfaction. We really enjoyed the time out under the trees, and by the time we saddled up the horses again they were raring to go.

"Whoa, boy." Daniel tried to stop Harley jogging and pulling. "Once we've dumped the Psycho Six we'll find somewhere for another gallop."

"And maybe some jumping?" Gable and I were up for more excitement.

"Okay," Daniel said, pretending to wipe his brow. "I knew you two would just about wear us out today."

"Yeah right." We were still laughing and joking as we crested the hill leading back to the clifftop, where we could see immediately that the group of six had already clambered up the track and were waiting for us at the top.

"That's good," Daniel said. "It means we don't have to ride down again. Oh, but something tells me they're still fighting—don't they look like a happy little bunch!"

I screwed my eyes up against the sun and saw what he meant. Jeff and Sara were once again in an affronted-looking huddle; Carrie was already hiding behind Ade and Dominic, using them as a shield between her and the approaching horses; and Georgia, removed from them all, was sitting on her bag, small legs stuck out in front of her and a defiant expression on her face. They said hi in a desultory way, then hitched up their backpacks and started plodding behind us. For a while we followed the faint clifftop path, with the glittering sea beside us and the long, lush curve of the bay ahead. It was unbelievably beautiful, but although Ade tried pointing it out no one responded. Soon he too fell silent and simply trudged along. Despite the brilliant weather the atmosphere was distinctly chilly and I felt very out of patience with them all for letting their petty, silly quarrels spoil such a wonderful day.

It didn't take long to reach Barrow Wood but by then even Daniel and I were quiet, the carefree time we'd been enjoying sullied by the dark mood of the group. We led the way into the cool cavern of the wood's interior, picking our way along a faint track bordered by dense undergrowth. I'd thought botany students would be forever stopping to examine plants and throwing Latin names around like mad, but this lot just marched silently. After about fifteen minutes Daniel turned Harley off the track and we pushed our way through a sea of waving ferns and bracken. I couldn't see any sign of a path or landmark at all, but after just a few hundred yards he stopped and pointed ahead.

"There's the orchid clearing. Ade, you've got the map.

Can you find your way back to the track and then to the road?"

"Yep." The tall, skinny lad had the page in his hand. "That's where Tam's meeting us. We just retrace our footsteps here and follow that track there."

"You got it." Daniel couldn't wait to leave them, I could tell. "Any problems, use your cell phone."

"We'll be fine." Poor Ade smiled weakly. "Thanks for your help."

We watched them move forward, still silent, their body language still registering complete discord.

"Whew!" Now it was my turn to mop my brow. "Now, that really *was* hard work. Let's get out of here—fast!"

Chapter Seven

I thought we'd be leaving Barrow Wood and heading for open country, but once we were back on the faint track Daniel led the way deeper into the forest instead. At first we just walked—the overgrown path, with its twists and turns and rampant vegetation, couldn't really be taken any faster—but then the trees began to thin and we cantered happily along a broad swath of spongy turf. The horses loved it and I felt my spirits rise immediately, relishing the feeling of escape from the grim atmosphere surrounding the group of students. By mutual, unspoken consent we avoided discussing it and concentrated on enjoying our riding instead.

"I've brought you this way," Daniel said, once we'd brought the horses down through their paces to walk side by side, "because there's a sort of natural cross-country course a bit farther on. Before we built our own I used to come here a lot."

"Great. There's one at home near the yard, just fallen trees, ditches, and some scrubby hedges. Gable loves it, goes round like a rocket."

"He'll enjoy this then, and it'll do him good to let off steam after all the careful practice he's been doing."

Ten minutes later we were approaching a wide forest clearing. I felt my pony's interest immediately quickening as his fine dark eyes took it all in.

"We'll lead the way to show you the best route." Daniel was having a job holding on to Harley, who clearly recognized where he was.

We went off at a good canter, slightly downhill, and popped easily over the moss-covered trunk of a fallen tree. Then a sharpish left turn to take a wide ditch, uphill over a prickly, red-berried bush, and then a long canter down to a broad, shallow stream. I sat very lightly in the saddle, making sure I didn't interfere with Gable's balance, impulsion, or rhythm, and kept my hands quiet with a light, steady contact. He was in his element, approaching every jump with total confidence, shortening and lengthening his stride in response to my aids, and staying beautifully supple the whole time. He cleared the stream perfectly, already turning as he picked up his getaway stride to approach the next, a very solid-looking bank.

Again I sat still, knowing how distracting it is for a horse whose rider fiddles around changing hands or seat, and was rewarded with a soaring, athletic takeoff as I folded forward from my hips. Two more fallen trees, then a curving swoop to double back, this time leaping over a shrubby bush at the edge of the stream, then cantering through the shallow to jump out, taking two narrow ditches and a pile of stones in quick succession. Daniel was just ahead, with Harley cantering easily and obviously loving every minute. We finished with a gently sloping uphill gallop and for the first time I let Gable go flat-out, reveling in the excitement of his power and speed. We caught up with the black horse in no time, startling Daniel who only just managed to keep Harley ahead.

"You're a devil-woman!" he said, laughing. "I had to call halt then or you and Gable might have gone past us.

I couldn't have that!"

"Yah, chicken!" I poked out my tongue mockingly. "Scared of getting beaten by a girl?"

"I'm not having Harley come second to *anyone*. So don't go getting any ideas."

"Just because Harley's perfect over your own course doesn't mean Gable couldn't win out here where it's natural like he's used to." The exhilarating ride had made me feisty. "Bet we'd beat you if we raced."

"Duh! Don't think so!" He was grinning but I could tell he meant it, and it made me even more competitive.

"Come on then, prove it. We'll go again, side by side this time, and I bet we're back here before you two."

For a moment he hesitated, but I knew he wouldn't be able to resist the challenge. The horses were up for it too, pulling and rocking as we held them at the start of the course.

"Ready. Steady . . . GO!"

Both horses surged forward and took the first fallen tree in perfect symmetry, to wheel sharp left to the ditch. Harley's turn was tighter, saving part of a second so he cleared it slightly ahead and increased his lead on the up-hill approach to the red-berried bush. Gable and I weren't far behind, though, and on the long slope down to the stream we gained ground, Gable's shorter outline and cat-like balance outweighing the black horse's superior length of stride. We leapt the water just ahead and this time our turn to the bank was perfect so again we reached it first, cleared it beautifully, and took the next two jumps at the same pace. We were still in the lead as we curved back to-ward the stream but Harley was drawing nearer, eating up the ground as he took the shrub and splashed into the water just behind us. We were neck and neck on the last three jumps, soaring over the ditches and stones, and sim-ply flying the long uphill straight to the finish. I really thought it would be a tie but Harley, with every muscle and sinew stretched, just got his nose in front and Daniel stood in his stirrups and gave a victory whoop. Gradually slowing, he turned to me, white teeth, black hair, and great tan making an irresistible combination of good looks that could knock you out of your saddle if you weren't careful. I managed to stay put, though, and grinned back.

"You won! No need to look so amazed!"

"I *am* amazed!" He leaned over and pulled my hair, but very, very gently. "I honestly didn't think we'd do it—you two are incredible."

"Thanks." I could feel myself blushing. I'd never been called that before.

We rode back peacefully through wild tracts of moorland where great slabs of sandstone reared their heads till at last on a nearby hillside we could see Tarag House glowing softly in the afternoon sun. It was a lovely sight—but the thought of spending the evening in the war zone that had become the students' company depressed me, and I said as much.

"Let's hope they've got over whatever it was bugging them earlier," Daniel said with a shrug. "If not then we'll just keep out of their way and let them get on with it."

That made sense to me and I felt great as we rubbed the horses down, then led them off to their paddock, joined as usual by Finn who'd been waiting for our return. Gable immediately found his favorite dust patch and rolled in it, watched by Harley, who, once his new friend had finished, proceeded to lie down in the same spot and roll too.

"Look at the state of him!" Daniel pretended to be mad. "Your horse is teaching mine some really bad habits."

"Tough." I picked up a hose and squirted him playfully so he grabbed it and gave me a soaking in return, making Finn leap and jump around as he chased the water.

We were still laughing and clowning around as we walked back toward the house—but I suddenly stopped dead, brought to a standstill by the sight before me. On the other side of Julie's pretty rose garden was a bench and there, book in hand, was my dad. He was listening, quite intently it seemed, to Georgia, who was talking nonstop and giving him (to my mind anyway) a lot of unnecessary eye contact. It wiped the happy grin off my face at once; it was all I could do not to stomp angrily away. Dad looked up, so of course Georgia sang out immediately, "Hi, you two. Come on over and tell us about your ride."

I hated the way she said *us*, making it sound as though they were a couple or something, but I told myself I was being paranoid and approached, though very warily.

"Everything okay?" Dad looked at me anxiously. "You

look a bit shaken; you didn't have a fall, did you?"

"No. The riding was good," I said stonily and Daniel put in, "We went round a jumping course. Tia and Gable were terrific."

"Oh, I could tell she was a fabulous rider the way she took her pony down that cliff path." Georgia tried to pet Finn and I was glad when he moved out of reach. "It's a real shame the guys spoiled everything by ganging up on me. It must have been embarrassing for you kids."

I hadn't intended bothering Dad by talking about it, but since she'd brought it up I said, "It all seemed kind of petty to us, just bickering really, but yeah, it wasn't much fun, especially when we came back after lunch."

"You see, your clever daughter noticed too, Brett." Georgia laid a beautifully manicured hand on his arm. "The rest of them turned a silly little argument into something pretty nasty. I was only goofing around but they wouldn't let it go."

Remembering how her face had turned ugly with spite when she was sneering at Sara I thought her version was way off the truth, but Daniel seemed ready to believe it.

"They did all seem in a foul mood with you," he said. "Was it because of the row in the morning?"

She shrugged. "Who knows? Sara was so weird about me hunting for the horse painting but Ade and the others were okay till we went down on the beach. Then they were so horrible I didn't even get a swim—had to just hide out of the way."

She made it sound as though she was the helpless victim of a gang of bullies. I saw my softhearted dad's concerned expression.

"I'm sure they didn't mean to be cruel, Georgia, but maybe it's not a good idea to spend time on the legend if that's what's upsetting them so much."

"I want to." She stuck her lower lip out in a pretend pout and batted her mascaraed eyelashes at him. "I think it's just the most fabulous story and I'd love to help you prove it was true."

I could cheerfully have wiped the flirtatious smile off her lip-glossed face and was maliciously pleased when Daniel said, "I don't see what you can do, though, Georgia. Brett's talked about the entry in the old diary to my parents and they're happy for him to look round the house for the painting, but they won't want everyone doing it."

"Oh, but I'm not everyone, am I, Brett?" She was laying it on with a shovel and I was glad to see my dad was starting to look embarrassed.

"Um—Daniel's quite right, in fact, Georgia. It's extremely kind of Julie and Tam to let me loose on their old books for my research but there's no way I'd expect to start turning their house upside down."

"Oh." Georgia looked downcast but then brightened. "It's a very old house—maybe there's a secret passage— oh hey, did you try the attics? Or maybe a cellar?"

"Tam's checked it all out, thank you," Dad said firmly. "I'll just keep on with the diary; the details in it are terrific material for my book so it's worth trying to get it deciphered."

"I can definitely help with that then. My father's an archaeologist, you know, and I've seen him work on manuscripts that are much older than this Creech kid's journal."

"It's kind of you, Georgia, but I really think you should concentrate on your own studies and getting back in favor with your friends."

"Great friends, huh!" The blond girl looked across to the Old Stables where the other students had emerged into the garden. "They just don't want me around so I may as well work on the legend with you, Brett."

She was certainly persistent. It annoyed me that my dad didn't seem to have worked out why.

He merely lifted his shoulders in defeat and said, "Well, maybe you could look at Ben Creech's entries for the month of March, which is where he records his brother's first sighting of the horse from the shipwreck."

"You bet! I'll take it back to my room and start right now."

"You're handing over the diary, Brett?" Daniel looked a bit shocked.

"No, of course not, the original stays firmly in your dad's study. I've photographed every page and put them on my computer. The old journal is very faded and been exposed to damp so the entries are barely legible, but they're easier to decipher on screen."

"I can probably enhance the script digitally." Georgia

was scribbling her email address. "Send the photos to my laptop and I'll do it tonight."

"Really?" My dad was so excited he just about forgot my existence. "Tell me, how d'you go about doing that? I've never—"

"Come on, Daniel," I said abruptly. "We'd better see if we're needed at the Old Stables."

Dad hardly noticed me go, he was so intent on what Georgia was saying, and I was so mad I felt like I had steam coming out of my brain.

"Slow down, tiger!" Daniel took my arm and led me to a quiet corner. "Why are you so angry? It's good Brett's getting some help, he's really keen on this and he's struggling a bit."

"Isn't it *nice* of sweet little Georgia?" I fairly spat out the words. "We all know what a kind girl she is, so she couldn't possibly have her own agenda here, could she?"

"You mean she's smitten by Brett?" Daniel obviously believed in plain speaking. "You only think that because of what Sara said."

"You saw her back there! Batting her eyes and flirting

with him!"

"Mm." He sounded doubtful. "I s'pose that's what she was doing."

"There's no suppose about it." I started flouncing off again. "And it's too gross to talk about."

"Okay." He caught up with me. "We won't then, but I think you're overreacting. Georgia's a windup specialist and you're doing what the other guys did—letting her get to you."

"As long as she doesn't *get* to my dad she can do what she likes for all I care."

We'd reached the Old Stables by now. Outside it Ade, Dominic, and Carrie were relaxing in the garden chairs.

"Hi Tia, Daniel." Ade smiled and Carrie jumped up and offered us a drink.

"No, I'm fine thanks." I was feeling too shaky. "I'm going to see if Julie needs any help."

I plunged inside, leaving Daniel to chat, and started scrubbing at a big bowl of potatoes that stood in the sink.

"You don't need to do that, love." Julie came in and gave me a big hug. "You're supposed to be on holiday—

the students are *our* problem."

I really wanted to hug her back and tell her I thought one of them was a much bigger problem for me but my emotions were in a horrible muddle so I smiled weakly and carried on helping. Daniel came in and tried to cheer me up but I was quite glad when Dad arrived and said he was going back to Rockrose.

"You can stay if you like but I need to sort out this photo file." He was so deeply into it he still hadn't noticed I was upset.

"No, I'll come with you." I dried my hands and said good-bye, but Daniel followed me out to our car, his eyes filled with warm concern.

"Don't brood about this, Tia," he said softly. "Talk to your dad, I bet you'll find there's nothing to worry about."

He was so sweet and I felt really grateful he cared about me. Before I could answer, though, Dad jumped in the car.

"Bye, Brett, I'll do it straightaway and I'll phone you." Georgia, cute in the blue cashmere top, actually blew my father a kiss.

I couldn't, wouldn't look at him, just stared out of the window as the blond girl, her hair hidden under her cutesy-wutesy hood, smiled and waved until we'd driven completely out of sight.

Chapter Eight

"Whew!" Dad was driving much faster than usual down Tarag's bumpy country track. "That Georgia's a real case, isn't she!"

"And yet you gave her our phone number," I pointed out coldly, trying not to let the swaying of the car make me touch shoulders with him. "Shouldn't you be discouraging her?"

"Because of the bad time the others are giving her about the legend, you mean?" He seemed totally unaware of the reason I was seething. "Sure, I don't want to be the cause of any trouble, though I don't see *why* it's such a big deal to them. As you know I prefer to work alone anyway, but if she really can improve the legibility of the journal entries it would be brilliant."

"And just what makes Georgia want to go to all that

bother?" It was too yuk for me to spell it out for him.

"Because, like me, she finds the legend fascinating and agrees it would make a great basis for a book. And she's used to investigative research, isn't she?"

"Her botany studies? The other guys study too, and they sure don't want to help."

"No, I mean her father's profession, which is all about deriving information from old artifacts." He glanced at where I sat stiffly apart from him. "They're very close. He's an archaeologist, you know."

"Oh really?" I said, heavily sarcastic. "How interesting."

"I don't get you, Tia." We'd reached the road junction and, suddenly angry, he changed gear noisily. "You're so moody. You seemed perfectly happy earlier and now you've got a face like—like a disgruntled camel!"

A great well of tears rushed up and prickled nastily behind my eyes. I turned sharply away so he wouldn't see and thought that however often we fight he never, ever makes rude personal comments. I could only think he was wishing it was the sweet, eager-to-please, cute, blond Georgia he was with rather than the tall, dark, emotional, and apparently camel-ugly me. It was all right for Daniel, telling me to talk things over with my dad, I told myself in a great trough of self-pity. Brett Carberry was either so wrapped up in his work he didn't have a clue what was going on *or* he was pleased and flattered to be the object of a pretty young student's attention and didn't care how I felt. I think I was too scared to find out which of these was true, so I stopped speaking altogether. We finished the journey in horrible silence.

I bounced out of the car and went straight to my bedroom to text Kate, wishing she was around so I could pour out the whole story. My best friend has a volatile relationship with her mum and we often have good bitching sessions on the phone, telling each other what dorks parents are, which makes us both feel better. Kate and her family were on holiday somewhere in Italy and we'd agreed just to send texts, so I made do with tapping out a vitriolic message about Dad on my cell phone. He knocked on my door while I was halfway through but I wouldn't speak and I heard him sigh and go back downstairs. I stayed in my room listening to music till hunger pangs drove me to the kitchen. Dad was cooking something that smelled gorgeous, and I had the horrible thought he might have invited Georgia over.

"Is that your special pasta sauce?" I asked suspiciously.

He turned and gave me his best smile. "It is. I know it's your favorite."

"It's—it's just for you and me?" I wasn't even going to sit down if he said she was joining us.

"Yes of course." He was removing some garlic bread from the oven. "Set the table, honey, and you can share a glass of wine with me if you like."

Ooh big deal, now he's treating me like a grown-up, I growled to myself, but I was so relieved Georgia wasn't coming I actually managed to smile back. The meal was delicious, and if our conversation was stilted at least it was amicable. We might even have got round to discussing what was really bothering me—but just as we finished the phone rang. Dad went into the other room to answer it and I knew, just knew, who it was well before he came back.

"That was Georgia." He was frowning as he took a big

gulp of the wine. "She got the file I sent her—you know, the photographed journal entries—and she's already started working on them but you won't guess what's happened now?"

"They haven't downloaded properly and she has to come here and use your computer?" I was tight-lipped again.

He glanced at me irritably. "What? No, of course not. She decided to work in her room because the guys are still being unfriendly and when she went to the bathroom someone sneaked in and threw water all over her laptop."

I blinked. "Why? Because they don't like her? Oh, it's not because of the diary pages surely?"

He shook his head slowly. "Georgia thinks it must be. She was using her computer for botany studies earlier with no trouble but as soon as she started working on my file this happened."

"So is her laptop ruined?" Knowing Georgia, I guessed it would be a real expensive one.

"No, she said she was already holding a towel so she could mop up the water before it went inside. It seems to be working still, but I told her to switch off and leave it."

"It was probably an accident." I just couldn't imagine Ade or anyone trying to wreck the thing deliberately. "Or maybe a stupid kind of joke."

"Or perhaps one of those students really doesn't want Georgia investigating the legend." He finished the wine and uncharacteristically refilled the glass. "In which case I should have stuck to my guns and made sure she stayed clear."

"You can tell her tomorrow." I felt a huge flood of relief Georgia would be off the scene, and decided not to tell him how worried I'd been about her getting too close.

"I will, but I must say I find it incomprehensible that anyone would feel this strongly about a hundred-and-fifty-year-old legend of a horse."

I shrugged, not caring as long as Georgia was out the way, and went to bed feeling a lot happier.

The next day Daniel and I agreed to start some cross-country practice as soon as the family chores were done. Finn, who was getting old and couldn't come with us on the longer-distance rides, always accompanied us to the little valley below the house, and I was making a big fuss of tickling his tummy when Dad appeared.

"Daft mutt," he said and Finn leapt to his feet in guard-dog mode. "Is he set to keep an eye on things at the jumping course, Tia?"

"Yep, we're just getting ready." I eyed his backpack. "I thought you'd be in the study."

"I'm taking a hike to one of the places I found mentioned in Ben's diary." He showed me the map he was carrying. "I'd really like to walk to North Cove where the horse swam in but Tam says I'll need a guide and it's pretty tough walking, so maybe another day."

Having ridden some of the wild countryside, I knew what Tam meant. I told Dad to be careful, gave Finn one last pat, and went to saddle up Gable. We warmed up for twenty minutes then rode into the copse, where I put my pony over a couple of small ditches and two of the big man-made fences. I made sure we got a good approach, using a straight centerline, and didn't hurry him. The competition in September would be timed, so we needed to learn how to cut corners and lose a few seconds here and there. Still, at this stage Daniel just wanted confidence-building clears, and so far Gable and I were doing just that. The only bogey fence seemed to be the pyramid of tires. My pony had been suspicious of it at first sight and although he'd got over his initial dislike of another of the jumps, the duck house, I didn't seem able to cure his reluctance about the pyramid at all. He'd dropped a hind leg the first time we'd tried it; Daniel thought the knock he'd received had taken him by surprise and put him off.

"I don't know how horses think," he said. "But I expect Gable's jumped the occasional pile of tires before and found it a pretty soft option. Trouble is our pyramid's built on a solid wooden frame with the tires slotted over heavy poles, so they don't move at all if the horse hits them."

"That might be it. We've only ever done show jumping, and the poles tumble off if you only just tap them. Gable didn't seem to be hurt even though he did give the tires a clout, but it seems to have put him off completely."

"You'll just have to be extra careful at this one." Daniel had dismounted and was climbing around the pyramid, while Finn stood on his hind legs, resting his front paws

114

on the jump, to watch him. "I'm trying to see if I can take this top couple off." Daniel panted as he tried to shift the heavy tires. "But even if I could, it'll leave the pole sticking up. That might be worse."

"Don't worry. I'll pop him over the stream, he loves that, and then take the direct route toward the pyramid. With plenty of impulsion and a good takeoff he'll clear it easily. He's jumped much higher so it shouldn't be a problem."

I turned Gable away and got him cantering at a controlled, buoyant pace. I knew it was important to keep looking up and ahead with my balance focused in the stirrups so that my weight was taken by my lower leg—not by Gable's back or, worse, his mouth. He was going beautifully and approached one of the natural ditches with great confidence, clearing it easily to canter smoothly toward the water. In this part of the valley the stream widened into a gully, forming a small natural lake. Gable loved to take the next jump of solid rails, land with a mighty splash, then take three powerful strides through the water, jump the upturned boat at its edge, and canter away on dry land.

We were now heading back toward Daniel, where he stood beside Harley, next to the tire pyramid, and I tried to relax and sit very still. Gable's ears were pricked as he approached the jump on a good central line, and I was sure this time would be perfect. Finn growled once but I was concentrating so hard I hardly noticed—then suddenly came the loud crack of a dry twig breaking and Sara and Jeff appeared literally out of the bushes on our left. I don't know if Gable saw them too, or if I inadvertently jerked in the saddle, but whatever it was made him shy violently to the left, nearly sending me flying from the saddle. Somehow I managed to stay put and brought my panicky pony to a slithering halt.

"What the hell—!" Daniel was running toward us, and if I hadn't been a bit shaken up I'd have been delighted by the look of total concern on his face. "Tia! Are you okay?"

I nodded, patting Gable soothingly.

"That could have been nasty!" Daniel turned on the two students. "What d'you think you're doing, surprising the horse like that?"

"Sorry, we're really sorry." Jeff sounded completely sincere. "We came in with Ade and Dominic to watch you jumping. I followed the sound of your voices and kind of lost the path."

"Sorry, Tia," Sara said contritely. "We didn't mean to scare your pony. Are you both all right?"

"We're fine." There was no point telling them they'd completely ruined our training.

Daniel was still scowling when Ade and Dominic appeared and told all of them to stay where they were.

"You're sure you're all right?" He led Harley close and put a hand on my knee.

"Sure." I smiled at him, having got over the small scare. "We *did* tell them they could be spectators. It's not their fault their timing was so bad."

"You'd better do some confidence-restoring stuff with Gable so he forgets about the tires for now."

It made sense. I looked over to the four students and said, "I'll do the water jumps again if you like, and you can watch Daniel and Harley do the bigger stuff."

"Great." Jeff looked as though he was still feeling guilty. "I'd hate to think we messed you up."

"We didn't expect to see you," Daniel said curtly.

"No, it was a last-minute change of plan." Ade shrugged ruefully. "We were going to spend the morning writing up our research but Georgia was driving us nuts about the legend diary. We decided to get out of her way."

Daniel was still touching me and must have felt me stiffen. "I thought she couldn't work on her laptop," I said sharply. "Didn't it get wet last night?"

"So she said, but she had it switched on first thing this morning." Dominic seemed fed up. "I was trying to work and she just kept on yakking about how clear she was making the script and how happy Brett was going to be."

"He's gone out for the day." I knew I sounded pleased about it. "So tell her just to send it to his computer."

"Okay." Ade didn't look thrilled at the thought. "Can we see some jumping first, though? We'd all love to be good riders like you two."

Suitably flattered, I put Gable into canter again and headed toward the mini-circuit we'd done earlier. He seemed to enjoy it even more this time, relishing the en-thusiastic applause from the group of spectators who clapped and cheered as if we were in a real competition. I then showed them the best place, farther back on a steep incline, where we could watch Daniel and Harley. This time I joined in the ovation as the black horse and his rider soared effortlessly round the course.

"Wow!" Sara was looking at Daniel quite starry-eyed and I was glad when, as usual, he came straight over to me.

"Thank you." He did a little mock bow but I knew he couldn't wait for them to leave. "Tia and I need to get back to work now, if you don't mind."

They looked disappointed but started moving away.

Daniel leaned down from his saddle and patted Finn, who was panting hard from following Harley's circuit. "Good boy, Finny. Get your breath back and we'll walk back quietly and see Gable jump this tire fence. Do it just once, Tia, and it'll give him a good memory of it before we leave."

We moved off and I turned to wave cheerfully as the students plodded out of sight. Daniel looked straight ahead, though, so I raised my eyebrows at him. "You were a bit offhand with them, Daniel."

"They're a pain in the bum," he said bluntly. "Behaving like a bunch of kindergarten kids with their squabbles *and* they could have caused a bad fall."

"Well, they didn't." I had a lot of sympathy for them because I disliked Georgia as much as they did. "Let's forget it and get on, shall we?"

Gable was more than happy to jump the ditch and then clear the poles to land in the water. He followed this with a confident leap over the boat back to dry land. This time, though, I could definitely feel him tense as we made the approach to the tires. I kept my right leg on a little harder so he wouldn't remember his fright and duck out. Just as I thought we were perfect, Finn gave another warning growl and suddenly, shockingly, a single, piercing scream ripped apart the calm.

I never, *ever* drop my hands but this time I did, causing Gable to lose confidence immediately. He reacted in exactly the way I deserved, by slamming on the brakes and stopping dead. I sailed over his head, hit the middle row of tires on their solid wooden frame, and dropped like a stone to the ground below.

Chapter Nine

I wasn't really hurt, just winded, and I managed to keep hold of the reins, preventing Gable from bolting off in a panic, so it could have been a lot worse.

"Tia!" Daniel ran straight to me but I staggered to my feet and croaked, "Someone's hurt. I'm okay so go and find out what's happened."

He hesitated then turned and ran in the direction of the scream, toward the heavy covering of shrubs to the left of the jump. I checked Gable over quickly, rubbing my shoulder, which was sore from its contact with the tires, and wondered dourly just what Georgia had done *now*. It had to be her, of course; the scream was just a louder, more strident version of her normal voice, and I was angry with myself for causing Gable's training to be wrecked again because of it. Finn had followed Daniel but Harley was patiently waiting with reins looped over a branch. I unhooked him and led both horses toward the shrubbery, calling Daniel's name as I walked.

"Over here, Tia."

I skirted round the bushes and saw him bending over Georgia, who was huddled on the ground making a noise I can only describe as whimpering.

"She thinks her arm is broken." He half turned as I approached. "It could have been her neck—look at this—I can't believe those four!"

Still slightly shocked by my fall I couldn't think what he meant until he pointed to a thin rope stretched tightly between two trees. "The other students did that?"

"Must have. Sara and Jeff came along this track and pushed their way through the bushes, remember? The rope wasn't there then, so someone's rigged it up to catch Georgia."

"But how could they know she'd come that way?" I was groggy but not completely out of it.

"They told me to." Georgia raised a tearstained face. "I said I'd join them once I'd seen Brett about the diary but

I couldn't find him and by the time I got down here they were leaving. I asked where you were and they pointed out which track to follow."

I couldn't think of a suitable soothing comment and suggested lamely that we got her back to the house so Julie could check Georgia's arm. She got to her feet with a lot of gasping and wincing, and leaned dramatically on Daniel all the way back, while I followed glumly with the two horses. Daniel helped her slowly toward the main house while I plodded off to the yard. I untacked Gable and rubbed him down, checking every bit of him to make sure he was fine, then did the same for Harley. I'd lifted the sleeve of my T-shirt and was peering at the interesting color of my shoulder when Daniel came back.

"You said you weren't hurt," he said accusingly, running gentle fingers over the sore, livid patch.

"I'm not, it's nothing." I pulled my T-shirt sleeve down to hide the bruise. "How's Georgia? *Is* her arm broken?"

"Mum thinks it's only sprained though she seems in a lot of pain. Carrie's just gone in to see her, and she looked pretty shocked when I told her how it happened."

"Yeah, she would be." A thought struck me. "My dad's going to go ape when he hears about it. He's already decided to stop her helping with the legend because the other students don't want her doing it. Now they've done this—"

"I can't believe the booby trap was rigged up to stop her working on the diary. Why would anyone care that much?" He was saying exactly what my dad had said, but I wasn't so sure.

"Why then? You heard Ade say she was driving them all nuts about the journal."

"Well, yeah, but tripping her up isn't going to stop her."

"It would if her arm really is broken," I argued. "And there was her laptop last night—one of them threw water over it once she'd started on the diary."

"They could be playing dirty tricks on her just because they think she's a pain." He didn't sound quite so positive. "It's more likely, surely. I mean, what difference does it make to them if Brett learns whether the legend horse really did exist? It's so long ago no one who lives on Morvona is really bothered anymore. Why would a bunch of strangers care?"

"I don't know." I thought for a moment. "Maybe I'll take a look at the entries Georgia's been working on—there might be a clue."

"D'you think you should?" He looked a bit alarmed. "I don't want anyone to start on you, Tia. I think you should wait for Brett."

"He's out all day," I started to say, but then heard the familiar voice as his footsteps squelched loudly across the yard.

Daniel and I shot out of the feed room where we'd been getting the horses' lunch, and gaped in amazement at the bedraggled figure before us.

"Thought I heard you." He smiled, his teeth looking very white in a face smeared and caked with black slime.

All of him, from boots to baseball cap, was covered. I could actually smell him from where I stood.

"Dad! Wh—what happened?"

"I fell in some mud," he said simply.

It sounded very funny and I think I was so relieved after the drama-ridden morning we'd had that I started to laugh. He pretended to shake his blackened fist at me.

"Such disrespect! You'd think I'd at least get a loving daughterly hug but no—all Tia can do is mock!"

"I don't think *anyone* would want to get that close." Daniel was grinning too. "Did you try jumping the ditch on the other side of Tarag Stream?"

"I did. I'd show you on the map, only it's covered in muck too and you obviously know where I was anyway."

"I fell in there once or twice when I was a kid." Daniel was unreeling the hose. "The ground looks solid but it sure isn't."

"*Now* he tells me." Dad resigned himself to having the worst of the stinky mud sluiced off in cold water. "Can you bear to let me use your shower after this, Daniel—oh, and lend me some dry clothes as well?"

"Sure, my stuff should fit, " Daniel said readily.

They set off for the house, with Finn staying well away from my still-squelching Dad, while I carried the horses' feed buckets over to their stalls.

It took a while for Dad to clean up properly. When he finally reappeared, looking unfamiliar and oddly young in a pair of Daniel's jeans and a baggy T-shirt, he was still very cheerful and upbeat. I didn't want to bring him down but I knew he'd soon hear about Georgia so I brought him up to date with the latest happening. I tried to make it as undramatic as I could, but even so he was clearly shocked.

"One of the others rigged up a trap and *broke* her arm?"

"Mum's sure it's only a sprain," Daniel put in quickly. "But yeah, the rope must have been there to trip her. Sara and Jeff came down the same track not long before and it was clear then."

"And this was after Georgia told them she'd made a legible copy of the diary?" My poor dad's face was creased with worry. "I just don't get why anyone would care about that."

"Maybe there's no connection with the legend research." I didn't believe this myself, but I didn't like seeing him so upset. "She drives the other guys crazy—it could be they're just paying her back."

"By wrecking the diary file on her laptop, then tripping her and breaking—all right, spraining—the poor girl's arm?" He started pacing restlessly. "I'd better go and see her to make sure she's all right."

"And tell her she's really got to stop trying to help," I put in swiftly.

He turned to look at me. "So you *do* think her injury is the result of her involvement with the legend? You just said it wasn't."

"That theory actually came from me." Daniel was always ready to leap to my defense. "I didn't think it was likely but—hey!"

"What?" Dad stared at him.

"Your fall today—you couldn't have been pushed, I suppose?"

"Pushed? Why the hell—oh, because I was out legend hunting, you mean? There was no one else around. I was following the route marked on my map and jumped the ditch into a boggy patch, that's all. Unlike poor Georgia, there was no harm done."

"Except it stopped you," Daniel said quietly.

Dad shook his head vehemently, "Honestly I just slipped in the mud. Look, I'd better go and find Georgia—will you two come with me?"

My gut reaction was to refuse, but I bit my tongue; I figured it would be better to make sure the persistent blonde didn't try to sweet-talk him. We found her in the Old Stables, alone in the big dining-*cum*-living room. Her arm was in a sling and she looked very small and quite pale, but obviously undaunted because with her good hand she was clicking away at her laptop.

"Brett!" She looked up and gave him a brave smile.

He rather awkwardly patted her shoulder. "More trouble, Georgia? I'm very sorry you've been hurt, but it underlines the need for you to stay well away from the legend research."

"No way." She lifted her chin defiantly. "Look at the fabulous diary copy I've made. There are a load of clues we can work with."

"I insist you have no more to do with it." Dad just couldn't help leaning forward toward the screen. "Wow, is this what you've done? It's fantastic, Georgia, I can read practically every word."

"Wait till you see November—it's a real doozy." Georgia flicked rapidly through the pages on the screen.

"Look!"

"Dad," I began, wanting him just to tell her to butt out so we could leave.

"I—oh my God, listen to this, Tia." He was now bending forward to peer over Georgia's shoulder, his face very close to hers. *"November 8th—Tam saw the shipwreck horse again*—something, something—*Chuckston Farm. His painting is almost finished and if the stallion is as good as his portrait he is a magnificent beast. Tam must hide the*—something—*from Father who is still very angry with him.* Unreadable line, then, *Tam's wanderlust and strange, wild ways are more than Father can tolerate. I fear my brother will be sent away*—something, something—*obsession."*

"It sounds as though the legend horse was causing trouble even way back then." Georgia was practically resting her cheek on his. "It's so intriguing, Brett."

"And dangerous." My voice was sharper than ever, and it snapped Dad back to reality.

"Yes." He backed away from the blond girl's chair. "I can't tell you how grateful I am for the way you've improved the script, Georgia, but Tia's right, your involvement seems to have triggered what can only be described as violence toward you. I shall make it clear to the other students that from now on only I will be researching the legend."

Georgia spun round to face him. "But I want to help—"

"No," he repeated strongly.

For a moment I thought I saw a blaze of fury in her eyes. Then she smiled suddenly and said, "It'll take you forever without my enhanced script."

"Without—?" He goggled at her. "But you'll send me a copy, surely."

"No." She mimicked his stern tone. "So if you want to use the readable version of Ben's journal you'll have to work with me, won't you?"

I'd thought she'd be tricky, but even I hadn't expected this.

"Don't worry, Dad," I butted in quickly. "We'll ask one of the other guys to doctor the file."

"They don't have the software." Georgia showed her small white teeth. "Or the expertise. I learned how to do this from my pop, remember."

I knew how very, very much my dad wanted to read the whole diary and was proud of him when he made a visible effort and said, "Then I shall have to carry on trying the hard way, won't I?"

This time there was no mistaking the look of frustrated anger on Georgia's face. She slammed out of the room, carrying her laptop awkwardly in the uninjured hand.

"Whew!" Daniel gave a long whistle. "That's one determined lady."

"It's not the name I've got for her," I muttered. "Come on, let's get something to eat and decide what we're doing the rest of the day."

We trailed back to the kitchen of Tarag House, where Dad's muddy stuff was whizzing round in the washing machine.

"That's kind of Julie." He stood staring at the whirling clothes, and didn't seem to hear when I asked him what he wanted in his sandwich. "Sorry, what? Oh, anything, love. I think I ought to go across to the Old Stables first and try to sort out this nastiness between the students."

"You can't tell them Georgia's stopped being involved,

because while she's got the file she still *is* involved." I was busy shredding salad leaves. "So what *can* you do—come down real heavy and tell them to back off?"

"Something like that." He looked gloomy, and I knew it was because he hates confrontation.

"D'you want me to come with you, Brett?" Daniel offered.

Dad shook his head. "No thanks, all this feels as though it's my fault, and now someone's been hurt it's up to me put it right."

He took a deep breath and walked away. I found myself crossing my fingers in the hope whoever was gunning for Georgia didn't hurt my dad too.

Chapter Ten

It was a bit of an anticlimax when he came back really.

"I told Tam here what I was going to do." Both men sat down at the kitchen table. "So he came with me."

"I understand Brett's concern." Tam helped himself to a sandwich. "But I didn't want him bawling those youngsters out so they all left in a huff. They are paying guests, after all."

"Yeah, right, but you can't have them beating each other up even if the university *was* your first customer," Daniel said.

Tam looked at him with irritation. "Don't exaggerate. They've just pulled a couple of stupid stunts on a girl who we all agree is winding them up. I don't believe for a minute they meant to hurt Georgia; they just wanted to give her a bit of a scare probably."

"And you don't think they're doing it because of Georgia's involvement with the legend?" My dad was still worrying.

"Nah. Why would they care? Whereas I think it's really interesting—the piece you were telling me about Chuckston Farm."

"Yes, that's right. In his diary Ben says his brother definitely saw the horse there, but I don't remember seeing the farm on the map."

"You wouldn't. All that's left is a derelict house and barn. The Chuckston family abandoned the place years ago. It's in the northern tip of the island and pretty inhospitable. The land is mostly patchy moor and bog, and it gets the full impact of our winter storms."

"Oh." Dad looked crestfallen. "I'd still like to see it, though. Maybe when I get a trip to North Cove to see where the horse swam ashore?"

"Maybe," Tam said guardedly. "Though I warn you it's pretty rough going."

"So where do *you* want to go this afternoon, Tia?" Daniel asked.

I knew the answer straightaway. "Can we ride over to the beach again and do some more swimming?"

"You really liked that, didn't you?" He grinned across the table at me, and I was glad his dark eyes still gave me that exciting bouncy feeling inside. "Okay, Coral Cove it is."

"What about you, Brett?" Tam was getting a drink from the fridge.

"More work in the study if I'm not in your way."

"No, you're welcome. I thought the journal entry where Ben remarks about his brother being in trouble was fascinating. Our knowledge of the family at that time is pretty sketchy, so anything that fills in the gaps will be appreciated."

"I'll do my best." Dad looked a bit fed up. "Though it's really hard trying to read the original."

I knew Georgia's computer file would save him a huge amount of time but I was really, really glad he was refusing to involve her.

As soon as the two-hour rest period for the horses was over Daniel and I got ready for our ride to the coast. This time we had swimming stuff and towels, and I just couldn't wait to reach the ocean again. Gable was much more confident going down the cliff, taking the steep, winding path as if he'd done it all his life. Within minutes we were ready, saddles and clothes stowed between dry rocks at the cliff base, and after vaulting onto our ponies' backs we walked them toward the sea. I let Gable take his time, and he stood for a while knee-deep in the turquoise waves, lowering his head to sniff, then pawing excitedly to send a great plume of water all over me. I shrieked with laughter at the shock but was warm again almost immediately as the sun's rays glinted and danced on my skin. The sky was high and clear with just a single wisp of cloud like a smear of ice cream on a deep blue dish.

Gable started moving again, wading deeper, and soon my bare feet were trailing in the cool, silky ocean. Daniel was ahead of me, and Harley was already swimming, a sleek, dark creature of the sea, cutting his powerful way out into the bay. Then, with only the smallest hesitation, Gable was swimming too, striking out strongly in this wonderful new element, taking me smoothly through the blue-green water that lapped around us.

"He's doing great," Daniel called. I saw him slide from Harley's back to swim beside him. "It takes some horses three or four trips before they take off but Gable's like Harley—just a natural."

I was laughing with sheer joy. Later Daniel said I looked like some kind of mystical sea nymph or mermaid with my long hair flowing as I was carried across the sparkling sea. It was just a fabulous sensation, and when I too slid from my pony's back into the water alongside him it was how I imagined swimming with dolphins would be, exciting, beautiful, and totally magical. Getting back on wasn't in any way impressive, mind you. I tried sliding smoothly onto Gable's wet, slippery back, but I slid off and ducked completely under the water the other side. I eventually managed to get aboard again with a combination of a handful of mane and a lot of undignified scrabbling. Gable didn't seem to mind at all; he was just swimming-and-loving-it, and it took quite a bit of persuasion to turn him round.

"We don't go beyond the bay." Daniel helped by getting Harley to head us back to the beach. "Once you go past the curve of those cliffs you're in the open sea, and it's a whole lot rougher and tougher out there."

As soon as we reached the shore I jumped down to give Gable's back a rest. The naughty pony immediately sank to the sand and rolled ecstatically, showering us both in fine golden grains that clung to every wet inch of us.

"He just wants the excuse for another dip." Daniel was laughing at my sand-encrusted face. "Go and wash yourselves off, but don't go too far."

This time I led Gable back into the sea and once we were both sand-free again brought him firmly back to dry land. He was obviously reluctant to leave this wonderful watery new world and I promised we'd swim again very, very soon. Daniel and I toweled both horses really well and I gave my soaked hair a quick rub but mainly just dried in the warmth of the sun.

"I can hardly imagine this beach in winter, with the sea all wild and raging," I remarked. "Dad says storms like the one that caused the shipwreck all those years ago are still quite common in Morvona."

"Yep, our weather can be pretty awesome." Daniel held Gable's reins for me while I tied back my still-damp hair. "During the winter when it's at its worst I still ride out to the cliffs, but I don't often risk coming down to the beach. Some days it's so rough the waves could drag even a horse out to sea."

"The shipwrecked horse must have been a hell of a swimmer then. I'd love to see the picture the olden-days Tam painted of him."

"Yeah." Although Daniel, like his father, kept saying the search for the legend wasn't a problem, I noticed he wasn't keen on me getting involved. "I'd leave it to Brett to find it if I were you, though I think it's more likely it was destroyed years ago. If it had been in the house some-one would have found it by now."

"Guess you're right." I had to admit I was starting to feel intrigued by the long-ago Creech who'd angered his fa-ther with his painting and his "wild ways."

"We'll make our way to Barrow Wood so the horses can have a drink." Daniel changed the subject so I joined in with the more mundane topic of music charts as we carefully navigated the cliff path.

After the bright heat of the bay the wood was cool and welcoming, and the ride back to Tarag House full of variety as we crossed open moorland and forested valleys. I was feeling fabulous, sun-kissed, happy, and full of confidence, so when I suggested one last circuit of the Tarag course, including the tire pyramid, I was deflated when Daniel said no.

"It's been a long day and Gable's probably tired," he told me. "Anyway I want him to forget that jump completely and we'll try a different tack tomorrow."

I stuck out my lower lip mutinously, and he pulled a hideous face in return. "Don't sulk, Tia, it doesn't suit you."

"Daniel!" It was Julie, calling from the vegetable garden. "Will you give me a hand to carry some logs in the house?"

"Logs?" He wiped the sweat off his forehead. "You're not thinking of lighting a fire surely?"

"Tam thinks there's a storm on its way." Julie waved at me in friendly fashion. "Did you enjoy your swim, Tia?"

"It was fabulous." I watched as Daniel rigged up a pallet to load on the logs and attached its ropes to Harley's saddle.

"He's an adaptable horse, one minute swimming like a sea lion and the next hauling firewood." He winked at me. "You go and untack Gable and I'll catch up with you."

I left him and started toward the yard but, still full of energy and excitement, turned Gable toward the valley and the cross-country course. He seemed as keen as me, cantering happily toward the first fallen tree and clearing it with ease. A couple of ditches, a log pile, and then we approached the duck house, its red-tiled roof glinting in the late-afternoon sun. Gable pinged over with enthusiasm and I headed him for the stream, enjoying the way he bounced over the solid rails into the water. The jump over the boat was the best he'd done and I swear I had no intention of jumping the pyramid jump, but everything was perfect as we cantered toward it and I thought, *Why not?* This time the only accompanying sound was birdsong and the gentle whispering of the trees, and I know I didn't drop my hands but I must have done something wrong because Gable shot violently to the right, ducked past the jump, and dumped me. The reins slid through my fingers as I fell and I'd hardly hit the ground before my pony had gone, galloping flat-out through the wooded valley and away.

I picked myself up, feeling a sharp stab of pain in my already sore shoulder, and called myself a whole list of unrepeatable names. I could only hope Gable would head back for the yard and tried not to imagine him turning north instead, to become lost and frightened out on the moors. I took off my hat and started plodding through the wood toward the slope leading back to the house. There was no sign of my pony although I kept calling his name hopefully. Then as I neared the edge of the copse I heard the crashing sound of running feet.

"Gable?" I peered through the trees and saw my dad charging toward me through the undergrowth.

"Tia!" He sounded so worried I felt instantly guilty. "Are you hurt?"

"No." I wiggled my shoulder uncomfortably but I knew the injury wasn't serious. "Have you found Gable?"

"Daniel's got him and he's checking him over. He said you'd be down here."

"I wanted to try the jumps one more time." I was surprised at how hard he hugged me. "Ouch, mind my arm, Dad."

"You *are* hurt." He fussed around looking at the bruise. "Did someone set another booby trap? Or did they scare the horse?"

"No, I just messed up, that's all. Daniel said not to do any more today but—"

"But you always know best." He suddenly stopped being worried and was just plain annoyed. "You're very stubborn sometimes, Tia."

I felt a great wave of anger wash over me. "I don't know why you bother with me then."

"I give up!" He thrust his hands deep in his pockets and turned away, so I pushed past him and stomped up the hill alone.

In the yard Daniel was washing Gable, gently sponging his legs and hosing the salt water and sweat from his body.

"I'm sorry, I fell off at the tire fence again. Is he all

right?" I tried to get my temper under control and ran my hands over my pony's neck and chest.

"Fine. No thanks to you, of course." Daniel was tight-lipped.

I wanted to scream. "Oh give me a break," I snapped. "I s'pose you're mad because I wanted to do the course again."

"Of course I am. It was selfish, Tia, you made things worse for your horse and you scared your dad."

I knew he was right, and that only made me feel more defensive. A tear slid down my face, and I wiped it away angrily. "Well, I'm honestly sorry that I upset Gable but I'm not bothered about the way you *or* my father feel."

This was so not true. The tears were pouring now and I really didn't want him to watch me cry, so I hugged Gable tightly then ran away, literally ran away. The problem was, of course, where exactly could I run? Tarag House was where Daniel lived, and the Old Stables probably contained six squabbling students. There wasn't another building, not even a shop, within miles, and anyway I had more sense than to leave the grounds. Although the

Morvona countryside was beautiful, I'd learned enough to know it could be dangerous out there, with wild moors and unmarked swamps. I really, really wished Kate was around or one of my other friends, but I told myself dramatically I had no one. Except, of course, Gable. At home I often told him my latest troubles—and anyway I wanted him to know how sorry I was about the tire fence.

Still sniffing, I climbed rapidly over the paddock fence and ran to the far side of the field to hide, somewhat childishly, behind the shelter. The two old geldings were inside, getting some shade from the oppressive heat, and they hardly looked up as I went past. I sat on the grass and peeked out toward the gate from time to time. Daniel was obviously being very thorough seeing to the horses because it was a while before he appeared. By then a part of me wanted to be more adult and go over to him, but a larger bit was still mad at him for being mad at me so I stayed hidden and waited. Both Gable and Harley were glad to be back in their field; I watched them take turns to roll and smiled as they touched noses briefly before settling down to graze.

There was no sign of Daniel or anyone else by then, so I walked cautiously across the paddock and sat down between the two horses. Gable immediately nuzzled me, his velvety lips brushing my arm, my face, and my hair, and I thought how wonderful he was to be so forgiving. Unlike my dad and Daniel Creech, I told him, and he placidly nibbled at the grass around me while I stroked his neck and moaned about how horrible everyone was to me. I noticed it was getting hotter and hotter; my T-shirt was sticking to my back and there was a sweat patch on Gable's newly washed shoulder, but it wasn't until a sudden fork of lightning lit up the field that I realized the sky above me was now a mass of black, angry-looking cloud. The storm Tam had predicted was about to break. I felt the horses' unease as the first ominous growl of thunder echoed round the field. I had no lead rope or head collar, and when I put my arm round Gable's neck to try and lead him back to the yard he shook me off gently and moved away. Another stab of lightning pierced the sky followed immediately by a great clap of thunder as the first huge, heavy raindrops began to fall. As if on a signal,

Gable and Harley took off, cantering together to the far side of the field to join the two older horses.

All four of them stood close together, safe inside the shelter, their heads turned away from the now torrential rain. I was already wetter than when I'd come out of the ocean, so there wasn't much point in running even though I obviously needed to find a dry place of my own. I sloshed my way across the wet grass and into the yard, where I sat miserably for nearly half an hour in the feed room, watching the storm crash and boom around me. Gradually its fury abated, the thunder became a distant rumble, and the lightning faded, although the rain still poured relentlessly from a slate-gray, lowering sky. The unbearable heat was gone; in its place a chill wind had sprung up and I shivered in my wet clothes. I'd done a lot of thinking as I sheltered from the storm, and sulking really did suck I'd decided. I owed Dad and Daniel a proper apology for my bad-tempered behavior so I stepped outside and made the cold, wet walk to the house. Instead of a concerned Dad and Daniel greeting me, however, Julie rushed out and handed me a big towel.

"Look at you, Tia—where have you *been*?"

"Sorry, was everyone worried about me?" I asked hopefully.

"There's no one here. Oh of course, you don't know do you? The students came back without Georgia. She went off on her own to look for a place mentioned in that diary of Brett's and she hasn't come back. She's out there somewhere—on her own and in this storm!"

Chapter Eleven

My instant reaction was one of genuine sympathy. Despite my dislike of Georgia I didn't want her harmed and hated the thought of the poor girl being out on the open moors with the storm raging around her.

"I'll help look for her." I turned immediately, but Julie grabbed me and this time wrapped the big towel right round me.

"Don't be crazy. You're soaked to the skin already, and anyway you can't go alone. Everyone else is already out there searching and they'll soon find her. Let's get you dry before they all come back."

I found myself propelled firmly toward a bathroom, where I peeled off my cold, wet clothes and stepped gratefully under the shower. The hot water was sheer bliss, and when I came out and found more dry towels and a thick bathrobe I felt a million times better.

"I've put your stuff in the machine." Julie was stirring something at the stove. "But I can't lend you anything to wear because you're so much taller than me."

"This is fine, thank you so much." I was quite happy snuggled into the robe, and when she handed me a mug of hot soup I felt the warmth returning to every finger and toe. The log fire, which only a short time ago had seemed a joke, was now crackling cheerfully, and I sat beside it in the cozy living room feeling more and more sorry for Georgia. Outside the wind had increased, throwing angry spatters of rain against the window, and the once blue sky hung dark and threatening over bent and twisted trees. Four of the dogs had joined me, stretching their limbs to enjoy the warmth as they lay in front of the fire.

"Where's Finn?" I asked as I tickled a few tummies.

"Oh, he's gone with Daniel, of course." Julie was peering out anxiously. "Finn's a bit old to be out in this weather but he wanted to go and he might be some help."

"Tracking Georgia, you mean? Where was she when she took off on her own?"

"About a mile or so the other side of Tarag Stream. Ade said he tried to talk her out of going but she insisted. He, Dominic, and Carrie came back by the long track while Sara and Jeff took the shorter route. They've all been back for ages. It wasn't until the storm started that they got worried."

"And they've all gone looking for her?" I was quite surprised.

"Oh yes. I know there's been some falling-out and nasty things said but they're all nice kids at heart and don't want Georgia hurt."

I thought about the tightly stretched rope in the valley and wondered.

"Maybe—" I stopped and listened. "Is that someone coming?"

Julie wiped the window with her hand and stared out. "Yes. Quick, Tia, grab some towels."

I tied the bathrobe more firmly and rushed back to the kitchen. Julie opened the door wide and we heard the full fury of the screaming wind as the storm lashed and buffeted the group battling toward the house. The outside light was on, and though it flickered unsteadily I could count nine figures and one dog.

"They've got her!"

Julie and I sprang into action, helping remove sodden coats, hand out towels, and pull off wet-through boots and shoes. The kitchen was a chaotic hubbub of noise and activity, especially when the four dogs left their fireside to greet Finn who, soaked almost to the bone, was unrecognizable with his thick, hairy coat flattened and plastered to his skin. After checking that my dad and Daniel were all right, I made it my job to towel Finn thoroughly, and when I led him in by the fire the old dog licked my hand gratefully. Georgia was the wettest person and with her blond hair darkened with rain and flat against her skull she looked very, very small. Her arm, in its now wringing-wet sling, was still held awkwardly against her body. She flinched and shuddered when Julie gently removed the sopping fabric.

"Georgia's frozen—she must have a bath in our room. Brett, you're the next worst—you have a shower down here."

It was true: Although everyone had soaking-wet outer clothes, apart from Georgia they were fairly dry underneath. But my dad's sweater was literally dripping.

"Sorry, Julie." He seemed very subdued. "You only just got it dry from this morning."

"You gave your coat to Georgia, I take it?" She was scooping up his things for the machine, and neither of them noticed the look I was giving my dad.

At last everyone was sorted, mugs of soup were handed out, and I sidled over to sit by Daniel.

"Are you okay?" I started a bit diffidently and was relieved when he gave me a smile. It wasn't the usual humdinger, though, and I worried he was still mad at me. "I'm really sorry I was such a jerk earlier on and I'm going to try my hardest not to be one again." I said it all in one breath. He reached out and ruffled my still-damp hair.

"It's all right. When you jumped Gable you didn't *mean* any harm, not like whoever pulled this latest trick on Georgia. Now, that someone really *is* a jerk."

"Trick? What trick?" I'd assumed the blond girl had just got lost.

"Someone followed Georgia and stole her backpack. It had her map, raincoat, everything. She set off across Tarag Moor but without the map she couldn't find her way back. Finn found her, thank God."

"Otherwise she'd have been out in that storm all night?" I was horrified.

"To be fair I don't suppose they knew the weather was going to change like it did. Even by Morvona's standards today's storm was a bit sudden."

I could just hear Tam's voice, slow and calm as he talked to the five students in the next room. There was a babble of voices in reply, and when he returned to the kitchen he was frowning and looking puzzled.

"They all deny following Georgia or stealing her backpack." He passed a weary hand over his face. "They sound completely sincere. I just don't get it."

"I'm afraid it's my fault." My dad reappeared, dressed in Daniel's clothes again. "Georgia wanted to explore an outcrop on Tarag Moor because it's mentioned in the diary. Someone doesn't want the legend revealed. I should never have told her about it."

"That's bloody nonsense!" Tam swore angrily. "If the legend's the problem, how come *you* haven't been attacked?"

I wondered if Daniel's concern about Dad's fall in the mud was justified after all but, feeling another wedge of resentment building inside me, I kept quiet.

Tam seemed quite sure the theft of Georgia's bag was just another stupid prank and said, "Anyway, I've told Ade and the others it's got to stop."

"Quite right, Tam." Julie nodded. "I don't believe for a minute they meant to hurt Georgia, probably just scare her, but she's absolutely done for, poor girl. I've put her in the spare room here, she was just so exhausted."

"You saw how wet I got and I was only out in the storm for a few minutes," I said. "It must have been horrible for her. Is it still raining now?" I was worrying about Gable, hoping he'd had the sense to stay under cover.

"It's eased off a lot." Daniel peered out. "I'll go and check the horses."

"Can I come?" I looked down at the bathrobe. "I could put a coat over this."

"Your clothes have finished in the dryer," Julie said. "Though I can't believe you want to go out in the rain again."

"It's for *Gable*," my dad said and smiled at me.

I kept my face stony, turned away, and went to get dressed. Daniel lent me a coat and we went outside where a few raindrops still plopped into a puddle the size of a lake by the back door. I splashed through and hurried across the yard where the drains gurgled noisily with the accumulated rainwater pouring into them.

"Slow down, Tia." Daniel loped beside me. "Gable will be fine. Why did you turn your back on your dad just now?"

"Why was it *him* who took off his coat and gave it to Georgia?" I burst out. "Why not one of the students? It was their fault she was wet."

I knew I sounded like a spoiled, jealous brat, but Daniel spoke gently. "He was the first to reach her, that's all. It doesn't mean anything."

"You think?" I didn't want to talk about it and pointed ahead of us to the field. "Oh, Daniel, the horses are out in the open! They'll be soaked through."

"If they need drying off we can bring them in." He'd grabbed some head collars. "Let's take a look."

He climbed the gate and whistled loudly. Harley's black head with its distinctive trailing star came up immediately, and he started moving toward us. Gable followed but the two older horses stayed put, heads down and grazing busily.

"Come on, speed up, Harley." Daniel held his arms wide and the black horse flowed into canter, mane and tail streaming as he moved effortlessly across the wet grass.

Gable gave an excited buck and followed and I spread my arms too, hoping he'd be able to stop before he mowed me down. Harley reached us first, coming to a neat halt a few feet away, but Gable, who'd done his best to pass his friend, was going too fast: He skidded sideways across the slippery wet ground and ended in a heap over to our right. I ran anxiously to him and was relieved when he got up quickly and shook himself, looking, I was sure, mildly embarrassed.

"You clown!" I flung my arms round his neck, which

was warm and dry. "He's only wet where he fell," I called out. "What about Harley?"

"Yeah, he's only slightly damp. They must have stayed in the shelter during the storm. I'll go over and check Dandy and Kim."

I gave Gable the apple I'd brought him, gave him one last check, then walked across to join Daniel. The two old geldings were fine and seemed to enjoy the fuss we made of them.

"Mum and Dad don't ride much nowadays, but these two still like plenty of attention and an occasional trip out." Daniel pulled Kim's ears affectionately before we left, and we watched all four horses drift away and settle back to their grazing.

We didn't see any more of the students that evening. Georgia stayed in bed in Tarag House's spare room, and the other five shut themselves away in the Old Stables.

"They're all very subdued," Tam told us. "So I'm sure this will be the end of their silly vendetta."

I still found it impossible to talk to my dad about Georgia and he obviously thought I was in another of my "moods," so again the journey back to Rockrose was uncomfortably silent. He went straight in and started on his computer, and I stomped up to my room and read the text messages Kate had sent. She and her mother were in the middle of an ongoing row about tattooing so most of the script was about that but in the last one she'd put *Yr dad wth a 20 yr old? Eeeyew. Gross!* Not very helpful but my sentiments entirely, and I just couldn't wait to get back to Tarag House, Daniel, and the horses the following morning.

I was happy to learn the students had already gone out, Tam having driven them in the minibus to some wildflower meadows farther south. I knew my dad was itching to explore the wild moor toward North Cove, but Tam had warned him not to go without a guide. I was sure Daniel would volunteer to lead the way, but there was no way I was going to let him offer to help. I knew it was selfish but I didn't care. Straightaway I asked if we could work on the problem with the tire fence before dad could get his request in. I guess it served me right when I rode out of the yard and saw Dad deep in conversation with Georgia. She was wearing her favorite blue top, had styled her hair and slapped on makeup and, apart from the arm in a sling, looked perfectly well.

"What's *she* doing here?" I growled.

I heard Daniel sigh. "She was feeling a bit rocky and decided against the trip today."

"So instead she's going to spend the morning flirting with my dad." I turned Gable away in disgust.

"Even if that's true, Brett doesn't want to know. Look at him shaking his head."

I glanced back to see the two of them disappear inside the house.

"Terrific." I was now rigid with annoyance, and Gable jogged uneasily.

"If you don't chill, I'm not helping you with this," Daniel warned. "There's no way you can do any jumping until you relax. You're making your horse nervous and we're supposed to be rebuilding his confidence, remember."

I made a huge effort and started our warm-up, doing some basic lateral work, half passes, leg yielding, and shoulder in. The first demi-pirouette was a disaster, with Gable completely losing the sequence of footfalls.

"It's because you're still tense." Daniel was watching critically. "Do some turns and circles until you're both completely relaxed and supple."

He was quite right, of course, and gradually we improved until, united as one, horse and rider were in perfect, sympathetic accord.

"Okay." We were working on a flat plain the other side of the cross-country valley; Daniel had dismounted and was leading Harley back into the copse behind us. "Stay there, Tia, we've brought you something."

I kept Gable moving to keep him warmed up and felt him quiver slightly when the black horse reappeared pulling a covered pallet behind him.

"More logs?" I called out cheekily but Daniel shook his head and made a sweeping bow like a stage magician as he removed the cover.

"Ladies and gentlemen I give you the biggest, the fiercest, the blackest—TIRES in the world."

"Tires?" I gasped.

The wooden pallet was heaped with the things.

"Yep. We're going to show Gable what fun they can be." He looped Harley's reins over a branch. "I'll build a very easy little course. I want you to jump every one perfectly and make a big fuss of your pony every time he goes over."

He'd brought a few poles too and soon rigged up three small jumps, all made mostly of the troublesome tires. I let Gable have a good look and sniff, then popped him over them, from right to left then left to right, with no problem at all.

"Great." Daniel patiently started dismantling the jumps and loading them back onto the pallet. "Now for the next stage."

"You're reeducating Gable, aren't you?" I thought it was a brilliant idea. "Getting him to forget his fright."

"That's right." He was panting with the effort of shifting the heavy tires. "And the way he accepted this little course means he's already halfway there."

"So shall I try him over the big fence on the cross-country?"

"No, not for a while yet. I'm going to add a few tires to the existing jumps. I'll put one or two on top of low fences, build a pile at the sides, or add them to the front of bigger ones. Soon Gable won't think twice about approaching a heap of the things."

"You're really great." I followed him as he and Harley towed the pallet back into the wood. "I'm the one who screwed up and yet you're going to all this trouble."

"Yeah, I must think you're worth it." He turned and gave me that heart-stopping grin. "We towed this lot down here this morning while you were probably still asleep."

I was really touched at the effort he was putting in and did my very best to respond and get Gable jumping with all his former verve and zest. The first time he approached his favorite fallen tree, now adorned with four or five tires, he hesitated briefly so I made sure I gave all the right confidence-inducing signals and was thrilled when he trusted me enough to clear it. We worked hard all morning with just a few well-earned breaks till eventually Daniel declared himself satisfied at our progress. We ended with a terrific gallop along a grassy track to the east of the course, then turned for home on a long rein at a cooling-down walk.

We laughed and chatted all the way and were still talking as we returned from the yard, heads close together in a lovely contact-making, getting-to-know-you-well kind of way. I looked up and saw my dad watching us from the garden, but as I was about to wave, a blond, sleekly styled head appeared behind him and my happy heart plummeted immediately into my riding boots. My cross-country trouble might be well on the way to getting fixed, but the problem of Georgia, it seemed, just wouldn't go away.

Chapter Twelve

Daniel had to go and help his dad with something so he didn't notice my abrupt change of mood—but Dad did, and for once wasn't going to ignore it. Walking away from Georgia, he took a firm grip on my arm and led me to a quiet part of the garden.

"Enough is enough." He folded his arms and glared at me. "I watched you just now, looking your best, pretty and carefree and obviously smitten by your new boyfriend. Then you take one peek at me and it's like someone waved a sullen wand—what have I *done* exactly, Tia?"

"Work it out for yourself," I growled and tried to move away.

He held my wrist again. "No, you tell me. Is it my book? You didn't want to come here, I know, but—"

"It's not the book."

"The research then? You don't want the truth about the legend—"

"Oh come on, Dad," I snapped. "I'm fine with the research *and* the legend. It's your choice of company I can't stand."

He was completely silent for a moment then said slowly, "Georgia? I know she's annoying but—"

"Give me a break!" I struggled angrily to free my arm. "Don't be so blind! You can see what she's doing, can't you? Acting like you two are becoming an item—"

"Whoa, whoa." He sat down suddenly. "You think that weird little girl wants—? She's twenty-three years old, I'm forty-seven, and we couldn't be less interested in each other."

"Yeah right." Although I was mad it was a relief to be talking about it at last. "She's flirting with you like it's an Olympic sport!"

"That's just the way she is. It doesn't mean anything."

"Duh!" I said. "You just don't know when you're getting the come-on."

"I may be old but I do remember how that feels actually. Look, Tia, you know how *you* feel when Daniel smiles at you or says something real nice?"

"Well, yeah." I'd never talked about stuff like this to my dad before, but today it was kind of necessary.

"Well, that's because he genuinely likes you and you feel something good in return. If I tell you there is absolutely no such emotion between Georgia and me, does that explain it?"

"Sort of."

"I promise you the only connection that girl and I have is the legend, and I don't even want that. I've told her unless she publicly announces she's given up the search, I shall leave Morvona immediately."

I blinked. I wanted him to stop seeing Georgia—but leaving the island and Daniel so soon was definitely not in my plans.

"What did she say?"

"She agreed straightaway, said she's had enough. Yesterday scared her, and it was horrible to see her trembling and soaked to the bone. She looked like a little white rat, pink-eyed and featureless without all that makeup."

The description of Georgia was cruelly apt and not at all what he'd say if he, to use his own expression, was "smitten."

"I guess you felt it was your fault she'd been picked on and that was why you gave her your coat," I realized.

He gave me a sudden, all-enveloping hug. "Tia Carberry! Have all these moods and tantrums happened because you've been jealous?"

I hugged him back. "Maybe. I don't mind the thought of you having a girlfriend, Dad, but not—not—"

"Not *that* one!" He laughed and hugged me again. "It just goes to show, the basis of practically every fight is a lack of communication. If you'd just told me—"

"Okay, okay. I've told you now. Anyway, let's hope because you've insisted Georgia quit researching, it'll be the end of the friction between her and the other guys."

"I'm convinced her involvement with the legend was winding the rest of them up," Dad agreed. "She's going to email the file over to me then delete it from her laptop, so that should cool things down. Come on, the wind's getting up again, let's go indoors before another storm comes this way."

The weather, which had been merely cool, did seem to be changing for the worse, and I shivered as the sharp breeze cut through my cotton T-shirt. Dad had wanted to take Julie, Tam, and Daniel to Redhaven to treat us all to lunch, but we'd all agreed to defer the trip until the students had finished their week's course. Instead we sat round the kitchen table and shared a midday snack with them, which in the relaxed atmosphere of the newfound understanding between Dad and me was really nice. Daniel and I stacked the dishwasher, and he looked out the window at the darkening sky.

"Another storm coming, Dad?"

Tam craned his neck to look. "Just the edge of one, I think. Hop over to the Old Stables and tell Ade and Dominic to postpone their field trip. An hour should do it."

I borrowed one of Daniel's baggy sweatshirts and walked over with him. Because of the building's design the front door at the Old Stables opened outward and was open now, blown by the fitful wind and banging dully on something behind it. A sharper gust slammed it shut, and I felt a tremor run down Daniel's arm to the hand that was holding mine.

"Georgia!"

Now the door was shut we could see what lay beyond—the small, still body spread-eagled facedown on the ground, her head covered by the blue cashmere hood. I ran forward at once but Daniel was quicker, kneeling beside the girl as she groaned quietly and started to move.

"Get my dad, Tia," he said urgently, then, "Don't try to move Georgia, we're getting help."

I turned and sprinted back to the house, calling Tam's name. The back door opened with a crash and he ran to meet me in the darkening gloom.

"It's Georgia," I panted. "She's unconscious. I don't know if the door hit her or—"

"Get the first-aid kit, Julie." He pulled a coat from its hook, and together we ran back to the Old Stables.

Daniel was still kneeling, talking to the girl, and he'd covered her up with his sweater but the blue hood was pulled away. To my great shock I saw a mop of not blond but soft, dark hair. Tam made no comment, taking over in a clinical, professional way to check the back of her head, then her limbs.

Julie arrived, first-aid box in hand, and said, "But that's—"

"It's Carrie, and she seems to be okay." Gently Tam lifted the small girl in his arms and carried her inside. "Daniel, will you ring Dr. Marks and get him to call?"

Julie followed him, and we closed the door behind them to stop it slamming. We hurried back to the house, where Daniel grabbed the phone.

"Did I hear yelling just now?" Dad wandered up, book in hand.

"It's Carrie. Tam and Julie are looking after her but they want a doctor to check."

"*Carrie?*" He went quite white. "But—"

"She was unconscious, lying behind the Old Stables door," I said rapidly. "It might have been the door that hit her but—oh Dad!"

"What is it, baby?" He put his arm round me.

"She—she was wearing that blue hooded thing of

Georgia's. When we found her we—we thought—"

"That Georgia had been attacked," he finished, and I could see he was shaking. "My God, what the hell is going on here?"

It was some time before the doctor confirmed that the injury to the back of Carrie's head wasn't serious and she only needed to rest. It was later still when Daniel and I heard exactly what had happened. It appeared Ade, Dominic, Sara, and Jeff had gone on their trip, leaving Carrie and Georgia working indoors.

"Georgia asked me to stay and keep her company," Carrie explained. "She was feeling low after yesterday and I felt sorry for her. She was putting her notes on the laptop and she pointed to the file about the horse and said she'd send it to Brett, then delete it. Then she heard someone calling, so she went out. I heard them too so I went to follow but the door must have slammed against me."

"But why were you wearing that blue hooded top?" Julie asked gently.

"My sweater was missing and it was cold so I put Georgia's on. I only took a couple of steps and wham—that was it. I don't remember anything till Daniel tried to lift my hand."

"Actually, all I did was check the back of her head." Daniel moved away and spoke quietly to his father. "I waited for you to move her. So what do you think—*was* it an accident?"

"Did they find out who was calling them?" I asked.

Julie shook her head. "Georgia ran all the way along the drive, convinced it was another trick. She said she was so mad she just wanted to catch whoever it was."

"So if the someone was ahead of her, they couldn't be back at the Old Stables knocking Carrie on the head," I said.

"Unless there's more than one person involved," Daniel pointed out. "If so, my money would be on Sara and Jeff."

"No!" Julie was shocked. "That lovely girl Sara? Impossible. I really think this time was a complete accident. Poor little Carrie ran outside and the wind slammed the door shut on her. Tam will have to do something about that door."

I could see Daniel wanted to argue but he told me later

he didn't want to upset his mother by insisting Carrie had been deliberately attacked.

"It's just too much of a coincidence with her draped in that blue thing of Georgia's," he said. "Despite what Mum says I know Dad's worried too, and he's going to give Ade and the rest of them a real hard grilling about it."

When the four students came back from their trip, however, they denied categorically being anywhere near the Old Stables.

"We left early and were on the far side of Tarag Stream when the sky blackened and the wind started gusting," Ade said. "Weren't we, Dom?"

Dominic nodded. "Absolutely. We talked about coming back in case another storm was on its way but there was no rain so we just kept going. Sara and Jeff hung back for a bit, but they caught us up later and after a while the wind died down and the sun came back out."

I didn't know what to think, but Tam's views were clear.

"I honestly believe them," he said simply. "I really do. I've told Carrie it must have been an accident and she thinks so too. Georgia didn't look convinced, she's actually gone dead quiet, so I said if she's worried she can stay with us in the house to finish her studies."

"Maybe she'll go home," I said hopefully.

"God, I wish she would," Dad said fervently. "I can't help worrying about the connection with the legend. Georgia was just going to send the file when the girls heard this voice. And that's a point: If there was a voice outside, then there was a person. Someone's lying. They have to be."

"It was probably the wind in the trees," Julie said firmly. "You've heard it shrieking, Brett. It's very loud."

He wasn't convinced, but like the rest of us he really wanted the accident theory to be correct; the thought of someone deliberately bashing Carrie on the head was just too dreadful. There was a very uneasy atmosphere, nothing to do with the Morvona weather, which, in its capricious way, had blossomed into a beautiful early evening. The horses had enjoyed a long rest so Daniel and I decided a short session over the new tire jumps followed by a twenty-minute saunter across the moor would perk us up.

The tire campaign seemed to be working brilliantly, with Gable thoroughly enjoying himself no matter where he met them. The sun was sinking low, a glowing red disk on the horizon, as we cantered joyfully along the main sandy track, which cut through the heart of the brooding Tarag Moor.

"We won't go far." Daniel slowed the pace in readiness as we approached a sharp turn. "And stay close, Tia. You've never been on this next path and it's easy to lose your bearings out here."

He was right: The dark moorland swept away to the north with no real landmarks, and the narrow trail we were now following twisted and turned and in some places almost disappeared altogether. Daniel and Harley, of course, knew their way blindfolded, but I could see why the Creech family insisted anyone exploring this part of the island had a guide. As we approached the house we could see the last rays of the setting sun gilding its lovely old stones and glowing crimson on the valley below its garden. I looked longingly toward it, thinking of the cross-country course hidden temptingly within.

"Can we have one more go at jumping?" I asked pleadingly.

Daniel shook his head. "No, the light's too poor in there; Gable might misjudge a fence and undo all that hard work."

I was quite proud that I didn't feel at all like sulking, just dismounted and got on cheerfully with Gable's evening chores. Daniel was good for me, I decided, being so responsible and reasonable!

We'd completely shaken off the uneasiness we'd felt earlier, so it came as another shock when we met a grim-faced Tam as he carried the first-aid box back to Tarag House.

"Before you say it, Dan, you were right." He looked angry and upset. "Today *was* no accident. They've tried again and got their real target this time. Another booby trap for Georgia, a great rock balanced on a door."

"What? Is she hurt? Is Georgia hurt?" We both spoke at once.

"Oh yes." Grimly, he showed us a bloodstained cloth. "She was hurt all right."

Chapter Thirteen

"It could have been much, much worse." Tam threw away the soiled gauze and washed his hands. "But because of her injured arm she pushed open the door with her foot. The rock only caught her on the leg not, thank God, her head."

I shuddered at the thought of Georgia's head being crushed. "Have you phoned the doctor again?"

"No, she doesn't want me to. It's a nasty graze, but superficial luckily. It was the police I wanted to call, but Georgia wouldn't have that either. I don't know what the hell I'm going to do about this. It's gone way beyond any kind of student prank."

"I hope what I'm going to say will help a bit, Tam." Ade, looking pale and shocked, was at the door. "Dom, Sara, Jeff, and I don't have any explanation, can only repeat it's not any of us trying to hurt Georgia, but we feel the only thing we can do is leave. Not just the Old Stables and Tarag, but Morvona Island too. We'll catch the first ferry to the mainland in the morning."

"I'm not sure about that." Tam scratched his head. "I think there's got to be a proper investigation before any of you go."

"Georgia doesn't want that. She's been weird as hell with us from the minute she arrived and now she looks plain terrified of us all. If she could stay over here with you guys tonight and maybe rest up for a day or two?"

"What about Carrie?" I asked him.

"She'll stay too. She's with Georgia now, the only one who can go near her." He looked saddened and confused by it all. "I'll phone for a morning taxi, shall I, Tam?"

"No, I'll take you to the ferry if you've all decided that's the best thing to do."

Ade nodded and hurried away, looking genuinely distressed. I knew my dad would be upset too and went off to find him. He was, as he put it, on guard duty at the Old Stables, waiting to escort Georgia to Tarag House.

"She's very shaken so I've persuaded Carrie to stay with her at the house," he said in a low voice. "Georgia doesn't want to be around the other guys ever again, she says, so what she's going to do about university I don't know."

"Don't start worrying about that. It's not your problem." I could see how troubled he was and gave his hand a comforting squeeze.

Georgia came into the room, limping slightly and nursing the injured arm close to her side. Carrie was with her, toting an overnight bag and the by-now-familiar laptop.

"Leave that here," Dad began, then glanced round sharply. "No, on second thought, Georgia, give it here. I shall take it home with me."

I realized at once he was speaking loudly for the benefit of the other students. On our way back to Rockrose he confirmed it. "I'm still afraid the legend file is at the root of these horrible attacks, and I want everyone to know Georgia no longer has them."

"So you're hoping they'll come and attack you tonight instead?" I was heavily sarcastic.

"There's a big difference between targeting a tiny creature like Georgia and a hulking great brute like me," he said grimly. "And you'll be all right, Tia, since Daniel's sent Finn to stay with you for the night."

The hairy hound was lying on the backseat, looking slightly puzzled but apparently content.

"Is that why I've got him? Daniel said would I take him home so he didn't bark and wake poor old Georgia up." I'd thought it an odd request but now knew it was Daniel's way of protecting me.

We reached the cottage and Finn ran straight inside and made himself at home. We hadn't eaten since our lunchtime snack so I helped Dad get a meal ready and put Finn's meat and biscuit into his bowl. The big dog stayed with me all evening, curled up beside me while I watched TV. There was a scary movie on and I was well into it when he growled quietly and I went suddenly cold with real fright.

"It's only me." Dad came into the room and Finn thumped his tail in recognition. "But you're being a very good guard dog, Finn. Tia, I've finished reading the whole of Ben's diary. It's so much easier on this file of Georgia's."

I turned off the film at once; this was definitely more interesting.

"And what did you find? Is there something you think one of the students wanted to suppress?"

He shook his head. "No, it's exactly what I thought—the day-to-day record of life on Morvona a hundred and fifty years ago, with just a few references to the sightings of the shipwreck horse. There's really nothing new—a few names of people and places that hadn't come up in other research, but that's all."

"But it's the first real confirmation of the legend, isn't it?" I said eagerly. "You've been hoping for eyewitness proof and—"

"This actually *isn't*," Dad pointed out. "This was written by the *brother* of someone who saw the horse, so it's still not a firsthand account."

"So what exactly is it?"

"Details of nineteenth-century life at Tarag House. There are several references to the Tam of those days who, unlike Ben, seemed reluctant to settle down quietly on Morvona. He was a bit of a dreamer, an artist who spent his days roving round the wild moors rather than working on the Tarag estate."

"It would be great if this Tam had kept a journal too," I said. "But, like you say, Ben's diary doesn't seem to have anything worth bashing Georgia over the head for."

Dad winced. "Not very delicately put, but I agree with you. I feel happier now the file isn't in Georgia's hands, though, and I'll feel better still when the other students have left the island."

We didn't have long to wait till that happened, of course. I thought I might be nervous overnight, wondering if someone would try to get at Georgia's laptop, but in fact I had no trouble getting to sleep with Finn's comforting presence at the foot of the bed and didn't wake till morning. Dad said he'd been a bit jittery but hadn't heard a thing.

"I'm taking the laptop back," he said, loading it carefully into the car. "But I've transferred the diary to my computer, and anyway I've studied the whole thing now so there's no point in anyone targeting it."

Tam had already left with Ade, Dominic, Sara, and Jeff

when we reached Tarag House. Julie was in the Old Stables, cleaning and tidying.

"Georgia and Carrie are going to stay in our spare room so I might as well get this place sorted," she told us. "Go on in the house and put some coffee on to brew. I'll join you in a minute."

Daniel was clearing the kitchen, looking slightly gloomy, but he brightened as soon as we walked in. Finn greeted him joyfully, bouncing up and down and wagging his tail.

"There's my boy! Did you do a good job of—of staying with Tia?"

"Of guarding me, you mean?" I grinned at him. "Yeah, Finn was great, even though we didn't actually need protecting."

"No trouble then?" Daniel raised his eyebrows. "Things were quiet here too. Ade and that lot came over to say good-bye but Georgia wouldn't see them. They all went off looking totally miserable."

"So they should." Georgia limped into the room. "I don't know what it was all about but they turned this study trip into a living hell for me."

"I'm sure they didn't mean to." Carrie had followed her timidly and made an obvious attempt to change the subject. "Say, Brett did you get to read the old diary? Any clues to that horse of yours?"

"There's another reference to Chuckston Farm—I'd really like to go and see the remains of that—and a mention of North Cove where the horse swam in." Dad couldn't help his enthusiasm.

I heard Georgia sigh. "I take it *you* had no trouble last night despite having my file? It looks as though you were wrong about the legend making me the target, doesn't it? I guess it must have been totally personal. Those four guys obviously just hate me."

"I'm sure they don't. I think it was plain silliness that got out of hand." Carrie sounded as though she really believed this.

"Whatever. Anyhow, Brett, you've got no excuse now. You should make your trip to North Cove," Georgia said.

"He has to have a guide," Daniel said. "We don't let anyone go in that direction from here unless they know their way."

"Can't I just follow the cliff path?" Dad was desperate to go. "I couldn't possibly get lost if I did that."

"The cliff edge around North Cove's headland is crumbling and dangerous," Daniel explained. "From here you can only approach the cove via Tarag Moor, which is dotted with boggy patches and longer stretches of swamp—very, very nasty if you fell in. The best way is to ride. Our horses know the area and you'd be following Dad or me anyway. We could show you the old farm *and* take you down into the bay itself."

"That would be fantastic!" Dad's eyes were shining.

"Yeah." I hated to point out the obvious. "It's a pity you don't ride, isn't it, Dad?"

Even Georgia smiled at his downcast expression.

"You only have to sit there, Brett," she said, and I noticed she wasn't bothering to flirt at all. "You could all go—Carrie and I will be fine now the destruction squad have left the island."

"A trip to North Cove?" Julie had returned from the Old Stables. "I think that's a great idea. Tam's been really wound up this week, and riding Dandy always relaxes him."

"Maybe we could do it when the girls have gone?" Dad was so excited he wasn't even worrying about the horse-riding angle.

"Don't wait for us." Georgia rubbed her eyes, which were, as Dad had said, very pink and rat-like without her makeup. "We've got work to catch up with, or we could have a girlie morning doing our nails and stuff."

"As long as *I* don't have to ride a horse," Carrie said fervently, "I'm fine with you lot taking a break."

"We couldn't leave you—" Dad began.

Julie gave him a gentle shove. "You won't be. I'll be here because you'll be riding Kim, remember. Anyway, as Georgia says there's no danger of any more tricks now the other students have gone."

I didn't think for a minute that Tam would agree to this slightly batty plan but to my surprise when he returned he was all for it.

"You're absolutely sure you don't mind?" he asked Julie. "I mean, *you* could go and Brett would ride Dandy—"

"No, Kim's perfect for a complete beginner and anyway I'm going to be pampered. Georgia's going to give me a manicure—Carrie doesn't want one whereas my nails would *love* a little glamour."

"Okay." Tam had stopped frowning. "It would take my mind off this whole student thing seeing as Georgia won't let me take it any farther."

"She still seems very stressed," Julie commented. "But it must feel better now the others are safely off the island."

So, to my bemusement, I found myself in the yard with my dad, showing him how to brush the placid Kim.

"And you'll need to pick out his feet," I reminded him.

"I've seen you do that," Dad said eagerly. "Do I say hup and he holds out his hoof?"

Daniel burst out laughing at the expression on my face and tactfully took over the instructions. It took a while but at last Dad was leading Kim proudly into the yard. Tam brought out an old chair to use as a mounting block and patiently talked Dad through the basics of how to sit and hold the reins.

"We'll put you behind me so Kim can follow Dandy.

Tia will be next, and Daniel will bring up the rear and make sure no one gets left behind or strays off the track."

Seeing my dad sitting astride a horse for the first time ever had reduced me to a mass of giggles.

Tam shot me a severe look. "There'll be no goofing around and definitely no bombing off. We may try a little trot but that's it."

Okay, so it wasn't going to be the most exciting ride of my life, I thought, but it was for my dad's research and this was my way of supporting him. Julie came to wave us off, and I could see a blond and a dark head at the kitchen window as Carrie and Georgia watched us go. It was a beautiful morning without a trace of cloud and only the lightest of breezes. I still had the urge to giggle when I looked at Dad's back, rising very tall from Kim's saddle, but I had to admit he was doing really well. I knew Tam had a lead rope in his pocket, but as we traveled farther north across the somber moors, Dad showed no sign of needing it and Kim kept moving steadily forward. The landscape really was bleak here: a vast stretch of scrubby heath punctuated by the odd rock, with here and there the dull gleam of black water marking the edge of a swamp. Dandy, his ears pricked forward, seemed to be enjoying himself despite the rough terrain, traversing the narrow, awkward track smoothly and with confidence. Kim, following closely, was also very sure-footed, but Gable stumbled several times and once dropped a hind foot into a boggy patch as we rounded a hairpin bend.

"Careful, Tia." Daniel brought Harley close in behind me. "You have to stay exactly on the path or you're in trouble. You can see why I don't bring you this way usually, can't you?"

He was right, it wasn't at all the type of ride Gable and I enjoy, but I was still glad we were there for my dad and was proud of the way he was coping with his first ride.

"Look over to the right," Tam called, pointing ahead. "That's Chuckston Farm. We'll be there in about ten minutes."

I peered across the moor to the gaunt skeleton of the farmhouse. Even on a sunlit morning it was a grim place, its broken walls rising like an ugly scar. The remains of a barn reared behind it, still retaining a few rotten roof beams above its crumbling stone. This was where the long ago Tam had seen the horse from the shipwreck. I tried to imagine the "magnificent beast" of Ben's diary galloping to this very spot. Even in those days, with roof intact and smoke rising from its chimney, Chuckston Farm couldn't have seemed the most welcoming of places. I felt a sudden shiver, as though something bad was about to take place.

Chapter Fourteen

I wasn't wrong, in fact, but it wasn't to happen at the derelict farm. There we just sat, watching Tam point out the rough perimeter of what used to be the Chuckston land.

"It was a croft, a smallholding apparently," he said. "They had a little grazing, a field or two, but that gradually disappeared as the moor reclaimed it."

"What would they have kept?" Dad asked. "A few chickens and a cow or two, I guess."

"Probably, and they'd have had to keep horses for transport way back then, of course."

Gable blew down his nose, impatient to get moving. Tam led us past the ruined buildings and out across the moor again. I could see Dad turning his head this way and that, absorbing the atmosphere and taking in the scenery that would soon be featuring in his book. He was amazingly relaxed in the saddle, and I was very proud of the way he remembered to keep his hands low and quiet. The breeze had strengthened, carrying the unmistakable tang of the sea, so I knew we were very near the coast. The heavy bracken on the moor was thinning, gradually replaced by the coarse springy grass of the clifftop. The older horses knew where they were, their heads lifting to take in the salty air and new buoyancy in their stride.

"Shorten your reins slightly, Brett, and be prepared for a bit of bumping." Tam turned round and grinned at him. "We're going to do a little trot."

Dad did his best, trying to relax and not collapse at the waist or fall back in the saddle, but he very quickly lost his balance, his toes slid down in the irons, and he looked like a sack of potatoes being bounced around.

"Whoa." Tam was still grinning when he turned again. "Better not keep that going too long. It's harder to do than it looks, isn't it, Brett?"

Dad nodded breathlessly. "I'll have to learn to ride properly so I don't hurt poor Kim," he panted. "I thought

I was doing pretty well up till then."

"You are," I said. "You've been great and you're gonna love it on the beach."

As I spoke we crested the brow of the clifftop and there was the ocean, glittering deep blue before us. North Bay was a much smaller cove than the others I'd visited, enclosed by the curving black cliff of a headland to the south and huge jagged rocks on its northern side. Gable was excited, prancing and jogging in his longing to reach the water, but when I saw how steeply the cliff face fell away below us I couldn't imagine how we'd be able to go down there to the beach.

"I told you it was a wild one," Daniel whispered in my ear.

I tried to look cool, saying, "If the shipwrecked horse managed to make his way up then we ought to be all right."

Dad, however, was looking down in absolute disbelief. "There's no way we can take the horses down there. You lot stay here and I'll slide down on my butt. It's my research, after all."

"No, we're all in this," Tam said. "Our horses have done it before. Just follow my instructions and give your horse plenty of time to pick his way down the path."

"There's a *path*?" Dad peered down and shuddered. "Okay, if you say so."

We went very, very carefully. My biggest worry was that my overeager pony would try rushing it and go crashing into Kim and my (I thought) incredibly brave dad. Thankfully I managed to keep some distance, and although Gable slid once, he collected himself quickly. We all reached the small, sheltered bay in one piece.

"It's fantastic," Dad breathed. "Can't you just *see* the legend horse's head as he battles toward the shore? Can't you just feel—?"

"Oh, he's off," I said disrespectfully. "Come on, Daniel; let's swim before my horse explodes with excitement."

We quickly took off the ponies' saddles and stuffed our clothes into Daniel's backpack to make sure they stayed dry. As I lifted the pack onto a rock I noticed four little round indents on the sand and peered down at them.

"What you looking at?" Daniel was holding Gable's

reins for me.

"These four funny little circles—oh, they're made by the studs underneath your backpack. I thought for a minute there'd been a small chair down here on the sand."

"Not likely." He laughed, then bent suddenly to take a look. "Yeah, you're right, the studs do look like the marks left by a chair. That's what I noticed in the dirt where Georgia got hit by the rock falling on her."

We hadn't mentioned the students at all—for which I was glad—but now I was intrigued.

"So what does that mean?"

He shrugged. "Well, I guess it means someone climbed on a chair to balance the rock on the door. It's just I noticed the marks when I went to see where she got hurt and I couldn't think what they were till now."

It was a nasty thought, the idea of someone clambering up with a heavy stone designed to fall on the blond girl's skull. I preferred not to dwell on it.

"Let's swim." I vaulted neatly onto Gable's bare back and he took off at canter, nearly dumping me on the sand.

Kim and Dandy looked up from the sea edge where

they were enjoying a paddle, and I saw a look of sheer envy cross my dad's face. He seemed to be thoroughly enjoying his first horse-riding experience, and I was pretty sure he'd be taking lessons when we got back home. *That's fine with me*, I thought as Gable plunged enthusiastically through the waves. This time there was no hesitation; he was swimming several minutes before Harley joined us and Daniel laughed to see the pure bliss we were enjoying.

"Isn't this *heaven*?" I called out, feeling the silky smoothness of the water rippling against my skin.

"It's not bad," he teased, bringing Harley alongside so the horse's fine black head was level with Gable's. "You definitely look more like a sea nymph than a mermaid, I've decided."

"And why's that?" Flirting like mad, I tossed my waist-length hair out behind me.

"Your legs." He gave his wicked grin. "They're too gorgeous to be a fishtail and way too long."

"They're only long because I'm so tall," I began, then clutched a handful of Gable's mane as a sudden, devastating thought struck.

"What's the matter, Tia? Did something bite you? You've gone really white." He leaned across to touch my face.

"We've got to go back!" I nearly screamed. "Not just to the shore, I mean, back to Tarag House. They're in danger!"

"What?" His face blanched too. "My mum and the girls you mean?"

"Yes." I floundered about, trying to turn Gable. "We might already be too late, we have to go now!"

"Are you saying the other students didn't leave the island? That they're still on Morvona and back at the house again?"

Rapidly I explained what I'd suddenly realized.

Daniel's quick-thinking brain went into overdrive. "It'll take too long, trekking across the moor. There's only one chance, Tia. If I swim Harley out to sea and round the headland I'll be much nearer to home."

I saw at once what he meant. "I'm coming with you! Gable can do it, you know he can."

"I think you should stay." Daniel, looking grim, was

already heading Harley out toward the open sea. "But I can't exactly make you."

The horses seemed delighted to be pushed forward, both striking out through the gentle swell and making surprisingly quick progress out of the bay. I heard a faint shout from behind us, Tam calling our names in an effort to bring us back to the shore. But there was no going back and even when the ocean started getting rougher, with choppy waves slapping against my legs and Gable's sides, I didn't consider it for a moment.

The difference between the calm, sheltered waters of the bay and the rough turbulence of the open sea was astounding, and although we stayed as near to the headland as we could, it seemed each wave increased in strength and size. Gable was still swimming strongly, but I could tell he was beginning to tire, fighting now to make headway around the arc of black rock to the south.

"Swim beside him," Daniel yelled, already in the water. "It'll help him a bit."

The ocean was several degrees colder than it had been in the cove, and I gasped when the first wave broke over my head. Still, holding tight to his reins, I swam beside Gable, encouraging him onward, both of us fighting to negotiate the curve of the headland and reach the quieter waters of the next bay. Daniel kept turning round to check our progress but he and Harley, being far more experienced swimmers, were gradually moving farther ahead.

"We're in the bay!" he shouted, his voice faint against the roar of the waves. "Keep going, Tia, you've almost made it."

On the map it looks a tiny distance, the little bit of ocean Gable and I crossed, but in reality it was the hardest journey we'd ever made. When I realized the strong relentless crashing of the sea had once again become a gentle swell, I was nearly too exhausted to care. Gable, though, took immediate heart, nudging me with his nose and swimming strongly shoreward. Somehow I slithered onto his sea-lion-wet back and let him take me through the calm waves to another beach, this one of stark white pebbles.

"Amazing, you were amazing." Daniel's dark eyes were warm and glowing. "I'm going to gallop home, you stay here and rest."

"No." In my mind's eye I could see the chair again, the chair used to balance that rock on the door. "I know exactly how it was done; I need to be there in case we need a confession."

"You can hardly speak, let alone ride," Daniel began, but I moved Gable forward and started the cliff ascent.

I still couldn't picture where we were when we reached the top; my knowledge of the island's topography was too hazy to work it out.

"Barrow Bay's that way." Daniel pointed. "From here we can get home in virtually a straight line, but you'll have to follow me again. There are still dodgy places on this route."

He set off at a canter and, feeling precariously perched on Gable's still-wet back, I followed. I saw the first ditch, wide and water-filled, just before Harley jumped it, and folded from the waist, missing the comfort and support of a saddle and hoping my balance was good enough without one. Gable flew over, his energy seeming undiminished as he landed perfectly to pick up and canter smoothly on. The track was wider than on the north moor, but it snaked and twisted through the same kind of terrain, skirting marsh, bog, and swamp. There were more jumps, a huge fallen tree, and, as we reached the Tarag grounds, a sturdy gate, but Gable dealt with them as though he'd been charging bareback cross-country all his life. Cantering on after the gate I heard Daniel shout, pointing to a gray shape hurtling toward us.

"It's Finn!" He slowed Harley a little. "Why's he out? Mum would never let him out while I'm gone unless there's trouble. We'd better sneak in the back way."

The house was just ahead, but Daniel veered away from our usual route to curve behind it. We were now approaching fast along a narrow path, and to my dismay I saw it was blocked by a bulky pallet.

"It's a load of tires," Daniel yelled, desperation in his voice. "I forgot they were there. Pull him up, Tia. I have to do it."

I saw Harley's muscles bunch and tense, lifting him high above the heaped tower of tires while Finn ducked through a narrow gap at the side. There was no way I was going to stop now even though there was hardly any strength left in my tired arms and legs. I urged Gable forward with every ounce of determination I possessed. My wonderful, brave pony responded brilliantly with a perfect takeoff, snapping back his forelegs to clear the tires with a classic, athletic leap. Harley was cantering on but Daniel's head was turned to watch us and I saw an admiring smile lighten the dark, anxious lines of his face. We were now outside the big vegetable garden, and Daniel pushed open the gate with his foot and beckoned me to follow. Once inside he slid to the ground and shut the gate, taking off Harley's bridle and letting him loose.

"Do the same with Gable," he said quietly as he made a big fuss of Finn. "They might eat a few of Dad's carrots but they'll be safe in here."

It felt strange, walking with him through the long garden, barefoot and clad only in a swimsuit. I could see a fine sheen of sweat glistening on his bare chest and for a moment found it quite hard to concentrate.

"I have to check on Mum first." The urgency in his voice brought me back to earth. "If she's hurt—" He clenched his fists and flattened himself against a wall, keeping the big dog close to him. "You look in the kitchen window, Tia, and I'll check the living room. If you see anything, don't go in, just call me."

I could imagine how he must have been feeling on our frantic journey back, worrying for the safety of his mother, and slid silently along the house wall to do as he said. Once I reached the window it only took a glance. She was in there, shaking something out of a small bottle into her hand. Acting on sheer instinct, I ducked out of sight and ran to the back door to burst inside and grab her hand as she lifted it to her lips.

"Daniel!" I yelled. "I've got her!"

She fought like a tiger, scratching and clawing to break my grip, and although she was only half my size I struggled to hold her still. The long, red-painted fingernails had raked my arms, producing long lines full of little drops of blood when Daniel sprinted in and grabbed her, pinning her flailing arms to her sides.

"They're unconscious. She's given them something," he panted.

"It must be these." I held up the pills. "I'll call the doctor."

She started swearing then, a stream of foul invective that poured from her pale, rat-like face.

"That's enough, Georgia." Daniel clamped a strong hand over her mouth. "It's over. It's all over."

Chapter Fifteen

Although he was right as far as Georgia's little reign of horror was concerned, the story itself wasn't by any means finished. The next few hours—with the doctor's call, Julie and Carrie's gradual recovery, the return of Tam and my dad and their shock at learning what we'd found—was hectic to say the least. During all this Georgia went from screaming hysteria to icy silence and stayed locked in the spare room where we'd put her.

"She won't say a word about *why* she did this," Tam told us. "I know you don't want to, Julie, but I'm going to have to call the police and let them deal with her."

"No." Julie, still pale and groggy from the sleeping pills Georgia had slipped her, was adamant. "Phone her father first, please, Tam. She must be ill; it's the only explanation."

"Carrie may want the police." He was pacing up and down. "Dr. Marks said she was worse than you and to let her sleep but—"

"I think Julie's right," my dad said. "Georgia's father should be here, especially if the police are to be involved."

"All right." Tam was reluctant but he made the call and told us Professor Soames would be here within hours. "He's flying in. He didn't seem that surprised to get my call; it was as though he was *expecting* some kind of trouble from his daughter."

I was curled up on the sofa next to Julie, with my eyelids feeling almost as heavy as hers looked. I was completely shattered; after checking the horses and transferring them from garden to paddock, all I wanted to do was sleep. I hadn't even showered, just pulled the clothes Dad had brought back from North Cove over my salty skin. Daniel had cleaned the livid scratches on my arm, and I hardly felt them stinging as, exhausted, I drifted into blissful, welcome oblivion. I didn't wake till Carrie came into the room, still pale and sleepy looking but much, much better.

"Are you okay, Carrie?" I made room for her on the sofa.

"Not bad, but—" She hesitated. "I didn't want to call the police till we found out why Georgia gave us those pills but—well, I think I know now."

She held out her small, slender hands, and for a minute I couldn't think what she meant. Then I noticed the band of paler skin on one of her fingers.

"Your ring's gone!"

"Yes. It was really tight, impossible to get off unless I greased it well." She rubbed the finger gingerly. "It's quite sore—Georgia must have yanked it off very hard once she'd knocked me out with her drugs."

"But it was worthless! She said—" I stopped and yelled for Daniel.

He and Tam, looking grimmer than ever once they'd heard about the ring, went to search the suitcases they'd stacked in the hall.

"It was hidden in Georgia's makeup bag, wrapped up with that necklace she always wears," Tam said when they returned. "Carrie's right—this wasn't just another weird prank—it was theft and the police have to take over."

"But Tam—her father's here," Julie, looking brighter-eyed, came into the room. "This is Professor Soames."

He was a small, quite elderly man with gray hair and a goatee beard, looking just like you'd imagine an archaeologist to look.

"Where is she?" His hands were unsteady. "Please, Mr. Creech, would you give me just a few minutes with my daughter before calling anyone?"

Tam nodded, then showed the little man to Georgia's room.

"Now you're awake, Tia," he said when he came back into the room, "can you tell us how exactly you worked out that it was Georgia behind all this? We were all convinced she was the victim and the other students were the baddies. What made you realize otherwise?"

"Daniel said when you both checked the last booby trap there were marks in the dirt made by a chair," I explained. "But that door's really low. Everyone here was tall enough to just place the stone on top, everyone except Georgia and Carrie—oh, and Julie of course, but obviously I didn't count her."

"Clever of you," my dad said appreciatively. "But that would lead me to think it must be Carrie, and you told Daniel at North Cove it was Georgia who was the danger."

"The first 'accidents,' like the water on the laptop and the rope between the trees—well, we only had Georgia's word. Julie couldn't find anything wrong with the terribly sprained arm that was supposed to have happened when Georgia was tripped. Whereas the injury to Carrie—the blow on the back of the head—was real and couldn't be self-inflicted. It made me see Georgia could be faking everything, trying to divert attention from the real reason by making it seem she was the target." I stopped, worrying I was sounding like some kind of conceited detective or something.

"Go on, Tia," Tam said encouragingly. "Had you already guessed about the ring even then?"

"No," I said honestly. "But I knew if I was right about Georgia we'd played into her hands by agreeing to our trip, leaving the coast clear for her to set up something else. Somehow I just felt we needed to get back here as fast as we could—though we still weren't quick enough to stop her feeding Julie and Carrie those pills."

"But if we hadn't caught her when we did she'd have taken a pill herself and pretended to be a victim like the other two." Daniel had done some deducing of his own. "She'd have told us her own necklace had been stolen along with the 'worthless' ring of Carrie's, and that someone sneaked into the house and drugged the coffee to do it. It would have been very hard to disprove and soon she'd be gone—taking with her what must be a valuable antique ring."

"I only paid a few dollars in a market for it." Carrie was still doubtful. "It was just a cheap copy."

"It was *Georgia* who told you that," I reminded her. "We can soon find out—we'll show it to her dad."

Professor Soames did, indeed, confirm that the ring was genuine. His eyes filled with tears when he handed it back to Carrie.

"It is worth a great deal of money and I cannot tell you how sorry I am that my daughter has caused such havoc trying to steal it from you."

Georgia herself remained sullenly silent. It wasn't until some days after she'd left Morvona that she confessed. We learned more details in a letter sent to all of us by the professor. He was deeply grateful that no charges were to be made, enabling him to seek medical help for his daughter rather than a court appearance. Georgia, he told us, had recognized the ring as an ancient original and tried from the first moment to get it. Knowing a casual offer to buy it would alert everyone to its value, she jumped at the chance to search for the painting of the legend horse as a decoy. The first morning, after failing to get it when doing Carrie's hair, she searched the girl's room, pretending to be looking for the legend. To keep up the pretense she also poked around in the other rooms, starting an ongoing row with Sara. The extraordinary argument on Barrow Bay was not, as she claimed, the students ganging up on her, but the result of an uncontrollable burst of temper on Georgia's part because Carrie told her she never took the too-tight ring off.

Reading this, it was easy to go back over all that had happened and realize just how Georgia had manipulated and distorted the truth to create a bewildering smoke-screen around her. Although at first she'd tried simply to steal the ring she'd become increasingly desperate, tricking Carrie into wearing her blue top before knocking her out so we'd all think the attack had been intended for Georgia herself.

"D'you remember how Carrie said she felt you lifting her hand?" I asked Daniel. "It must have been Georgia trying to tear that ring off her finger—only we came along and she had to run."

"It's unbelievable." Dad put down the letter and shuddered. "Georgia turned herself into a monster because she wanted the ring so much, and yet she didn't need the money. We all knew how rich she was with her continual shopping for designer clothes and shoes."

"Ah." Tam showed him the last page. "Look at this—her father says she's had a problem for years with compulsive spending and he told her he'd no longer bail her out when the bills mounted up. She said she'd destroy all her credit cards."

"But she didn't, she just carried on shopping." Julie

216

looked down at her comfortably scruffy jeans. "Oh, I'd much rather look like this and not be thousands in debt."

We all laughed at that. I said mockingly to Dad, "All that fretting about it being your fault for getting Georgia involved and the grubby truth is—it was all about money and greed."

"And all that flirting you thought was just for me was only part of her complicated smokescreen," he retaliated. "I guess she fooled everyone at one time."

"But thanks to Super Tia and her Super Horse, Georgia got found out in the end," Daniel said. "Speaking of which, d'you want a practice spin round the cross-country course?" Tam had brought back our saddles hooked together slung over his patient gelding's haunches like saddlebags.

"Ooh yeah," I said eagerly. "I just love it now Gable's a hundred percent with *all* the fences. Daniel had a whole load more tires to take to the course, Dad, but Gable jumped them all in one go and he's perfect now."

I didn't add that we'd actually cleared the tires bareback and half naked—no point in worrying him, I'm sure you'll agree.

"Before you go—Daniel. could you help me cement that big stone back into the Old Stable's wall?" Tam asked. "It's the one Georgia used to set up her booby trap. It's been loose for ages but I didn't get round to fixing it. I only need you to hold it in place—five minutes at the most."

They went off while Dad and I finished our coffee and watched Julie carefully fold away the professor's letter.

"Poor old man," she sighed. "It's going to take a lot to get Georgia back on the straight and narrow. I think he must have spoiled that girl badly when she was little."

I privately thought Georgia was just one of nature's bad seeds, but Julie was so sweet I didn't say so. Just as we were about to leave the kitchen Tam, Daniel, and of course Finn rushed back in.

"Look, Brett, look!" Tam was nearly incoherent. "Daniel swept out the cavity where the loose stone came from and found this!"

Reverently, Dad took the leather-bound book and a roll of old canvas. "It's another journal—just like Ben's but this one's in better condition." He opened the old book at the last entry.

"November 20th. Today I saw the horse from the wrecked ship again, leaping the fence from Chuckston Farm's pasture. It is not only his beauty but his wild nature and perfect freedom I envy. I leave for the docks at first light. I shall miss my brother but not this island. The world will become my new home."

There was a hushed silence in the room as we tried to take it in.

"So you were right—the horse *did* exist, Brett," Tam said softly. "And he inspired my ancestor to seek his own greener pastures, as it were."

It was strange, thinking of the long-ago youngster running away from home to seek his fortune.

"The legend horse must have left his mark on Morvona's horse population," Julie pointed out. "Daniel always thought somewhere along the line there was some real quality. The Chuckston Farm mares got a visit from the shipwrecked stallion, and I daresay others did too."

"Well!" Tam, to our surprise, began to laugh. "There's no doubt in my mind anymore that the stallion was here."

He finished unrolling the canvas and held it up for us

to see. It was the missing painting—amateurly done but still devastating. It showed the horse of the legend, standing proudly against the somber background of Tarag Moor. He was beautiful, with classic lines and a noble strength, a true, deep black in color. And there, poignantly familiar, was a white star on his brow—a white star with an unusually long trailing point running almost to the tip of his nose.

"My God!" Dad looked stunned. "He looks just like Harley!"

I could see the emotion on Daniel's face as he gazed at the hundred-and-fifty-year-old picture. He turned to look at me and said, in a shy but proud kind of voice, "Now I've got *two* reasons to be glad you came here!"